William Jackson

Thirty Letters on Various Subjects

Third Edition

William Jackson

Thirty Letters on Various Subjects
Third Edition

ISBN/EAN: 9783744716154

Printed in Europe, USA, Canada, Australia, Japan

Cover: Foto ©Andreas Hilbeck / pixelio.de

More available books at **www.hansebooks.com**

THIRTY

LETTERS

ON

VARIOUS SUBJECTS.

BY

WILLIAM JACKSON.

THE THIRD EDITION,

WITH CONSIDERABLE ADDITIONS.

LONDON:

PRINTED FOR T. CADELL, JUN. AND W. DAVIES,

(SUCCESSORS TO MR. CADELL)

IN THE STRAND.

1795.

ADVERTISEMENT.

WHEN an unknown author prefents his work to the public, the form of Letters has fome advantages: It feems to excufe deep definition, and admits of a loofenefs of ftyle as properly fuited to an epiftolary correfpondence. But when it is difcovered that the letters are not real, the reader is lefs difpofed to make allowances.—He expects greater regularity and more correctnefs. The author, confcious of thefe expectations, in endeavouring not to difappoint them, abates of his familiarity, and arranges his arguments ; which, not agreeing with the freedom of the firft defign, his book becomes a kind of mongrel performance—more correct, but lefs characteriftic.

Notwithstanding the above remark, in other respects this will be found superior to the first and second editions—many passages have been omitted which might always have been spared, but more have been added to subjects treated too briefly. One letter is entirely new.

Upon the revisal of this work, some expressions were found innocent which have incurred censure, and others really faulty which have escaped it—the latter it is hoped are amended; but in respect of the former, permit me to say, in the words of a late writer—" Pour toute réponse, j'ai étendu mes idées et mes reflections en les frappant d'une manière plus haute et plus décidée; laissant au temps, dont je connois les effets, le foin de mettre mes opinions à leur place."

LETTER

CONTENTS.

LETTERS.

LETTER I.

SINCE you requeſt that our correſpondence ſhould be out of the beaten track, be it ſo. My retirement from the world will naturally give an air of peculiarity to my ſentiments, which perhaps may entertain where it does not convince.

In juſtice to myſelf, let me obſerve, that truth ſometimes does not ſtrike us without the aſſiſtance of cuſtom; but ſo great is the force of cuſtom, that, unaſſiſted by truth, it has worked the greateſt miracles. Need I bring for proof the quantity of nonſenſe in all the arts, ſciences, and even religion itſelf, which it has ſanctified ?

B   As

As poffibly in the courfe of my letters
to you I may attack fome received doc-
trines on each of thefe fubjects, let not
what I advance be inftantly rejected, becaufe contrary to an opinion founded on
prejudice ; but, as much as poffible, diveft yourfelf of the partiality acquired by
habit, and if at laft you fhould not agree
with me, I fhall fufpect my fentiments
to be peculiar, and not juft.

Tho' truth may want the affiftance of
ufe before we feel its force, yet when it is
really felt, we reject what cuftom only
made us approve. The difficulty is to
procure for truth a fair examination.
The multitude is always againft it. The
firft difcovery in any thing is confidered
as an encroachment upon property, a property become facred by poffeffion. Dif-
coverers are accordingly treated as crimi-
nals, and muft have good luck to efcape
execution.

I mean

I mean not to rank myfelf with fuch bold adventurers ; I am neither ambitious of the honour, nor the danger, of en-lightening the world; but if I can foften prejudices which I cannot remove—if I can loofen the fetters of cuftom where I cannot altogether unbind them, and en-gage you to think for yourfelf—my end will be anfwered, and my trouble fully repaid.

Adieu! &c.

LETTER

LETTER II.

*   *   *   *   *   *.

IT is natural to fuppofe, that people originally judged of things by their fenfes and immediate perceptions. By degrees they found that their fenfes were not infallible, and that things frequently contradicted their firft appearance.

This, at laft, was pufhed to an extravagance; and certain philofophers endeavoured to perfuade mankind, that the fenfes deceive us fo often, that we can never depend on them—that we cannot tell whether we are in motion or at reft, afleep or awake, with many other fuch abfurdities.

They ufed the fame ingenuity with the mental fenfe. Some ancient fage was afked,

afked, " Who is the richeft man?" If
he had replied, " He that has moft
money," the anfwer would have been
natural and juft—what he did fay every
one knows. We have fuffered ourfelves
to be impofed on fo long, that at laft we
begin to impofe on ourfelves.

Riches, cards, and duelling, have fur-
nifhed conftant topics for abufe, to di-
vines and moralifts; and yet men will
ftill hoard, play, and fight. Why fhould
we obey our feelings rather than precepts
perpetually inculcated?

All univerfal paffions we may fairly
pronounce to be natural, and fhould be
treated with refpect. The gratification
of our paffions are our greateft pleafures,
and he that has moft gratifications is of
courfe the happieft man. This, as a general affertion, is true, and it is true alfo
in particulars; provided we pay no more
for pleafure than it is worth.

Every

Every man should endeavour to be
rich. He that has money may poffefs
every thing that is transferable—this is a
fufficient inducement to procure it. Nay,
if he poffeffes nothing but his money,
if he confiders it as the end, as well as
the means, it is ftill right to be rich ; for,
knowing that he has it in his power to
procure every thing, he is as well fatisfied as if the thing itfelf was in his poffeffion.

This is the true fource of the mifer's
pleafure ; and a great pleafure it is ! A
moral philofopher may tell him, " that
man does not live for himfelf alone, and
that he hurts the community by with-
holding what would be of ufe to it"—
this he thinks to be weak reafoning. The
fneers of wits fignify as little ; for he
knows they would be glad to be rich if
they could. He feels that the pleafure
arifing from the poffeffion of riches, whether ufed or not, is too great to be given
up

up for all the ridicule, or even the ſtrong-
eſt arguments that can be brought againſt
it.

If ſo much may be ſaid in defence of
avarice as a general principle, much more
may be advanced in its favour when it is
the paſſion of age. It is a natural
wiſh to enjoy ſomething.—Love is our
purſuit in youth—ambition in middle
life—there is nothing left for an old man,
but the deſire of poſſeſſing money; of
which he is as jealous as he ever was of
his miſtreſs, and moſt unwillingly reſigns
it to his ſucceſſor, whom he conſiders as
his rival.

It ſeems to be agreed, that card-play-
ing proceeds entirely from avarice—tho'
this may ſometimes be the motive, yet it
may with more probability be derived
from other, and more general principles.

The

The mind of man naturally requires employment, and that employment is moſt agreeable, which engages, without fatiguing the attention. There is nothing for this purpoſe of ſuch univerſal attraction as cards. The fine arts and belles lettres can only be enjoyed by thoſe who have a genius for them—other ſtudies and amuſements have their particular charm, but cards are the univerſal amuſement in every country where they are known.— The alternate changes in the play, the hope upon the taking up a new hand, and the triumph of getting a game, made more compleat from the fear of loſing it, keep the mind in a perpetual agitation, which is found by experience to be too agreeable to be quitted for any other conſideration. The ſtake played for is a quickener of theſe ſenſations, but not the cauſe. Children who play for nothing, feel what I have been deſcribing, perhaps in a more exquiſite degree, than thoſe who game for thouſands. A ſtate of inaction is

of

of all others the moft dreadful! and it is
to avoid this inaction that we feek employment, though at the expence of
health, temper, and fortune.

This fubject is finely touched by Abbé
du Bos, in his reflexions upon poetry,
&c. indeed he carries it fo far as to fay,
that the pleafure arifing from an extraor-
dinary agitation of the mind, is frequently
fo great as to ftifle humanity ; and from
hence arifes the entertainment of the common people at executions, and of the
better fort at tragedies. Although in this
laft inftance he may be miftaken ; yet,
the delight we feel in reading the actions
of a hero may be referred to this caufe.
The moralift cenfures the tafte of thofe
who can be pleafed with the actions of
an Alexander or a Nadir Shah—the Truth
is, we do not approve the actions ; but
the relation of them caufes that agitation
of the mind which we find to be fo pleafant. The reign of Henry the feventh,
tho'

tho' of the greateſt conſequence to this
nation, does not intereſt us like the con-
tentions of York and Lancaſter, by which
the kingdom was ruined. In vain are we
told that ſcenes of war and bloodſhed can
give no pleaſure to a good mind, and that
the true hero is he who cultivates the arts
of peace, whoſe ſtudies and employments
confer benefits on mankind, not procure
their deſtruction, It is to no purpoſe—
we ſleep over the actions of quiet good-
neſs; while aſpiring, deſtroying greatneſs,
claims and commands our attention *.

Duelling has in many countries a law
againſt it—but will never be prevented.

ℜ   The

---

* A great writer has remarked that " the exploits
of conquerors who have deſolated the earth, and the
freaks of tyrants who have rendered nations unhappy, are recorded with minute, and often *diſguſt-
ing* accuracy, while the diſcovery of uſeful arts, and
the

The law can inflict no greater penalty for
any breach of it than death ; which the
duellift contemns.—There are alfo fome
cafes of injury which laws cannot prevent, nor punifh when committed—thefe
muft be redreffed by the man who fuffers,
and by him *only*, He is prompted to do
this by fomething antecedent, and fuperior to all law, and by a defire as eager
as hunger or luft ; fo that it is as eafy for
laws to prevent or reftrain the two latter
as the former. Very luckily for us, occafions for the gratifications of this paffion occur but feldom ; and tho' a man
may be reftrained from a duel by perfonal
fear, which is its only counteractor, there

the progrefs of the moft beneficial branches of com-
merce are paffed over in filence and fuffered to fink
into oblivion. The preceding obfervations may
fhew that we are not *difgufted*, but, on the contrary,
much interefted and delighted by the accuracy and
minutenefs of fuch records. Perhaps the warm affertion of a great military character, tho' enthufiaftic,
is not far beyond the truth.—" War calls forth the
nobleft feelings of the human heart."

are

are very few instances, perhaps none, of its being prevented by considering it as a breach of the law.

In the beginning of the last century duels were so frequent, particularly in France, as to occasion a severe edict to prevent them—indeed by their frequency, they were by degrees improved into combats of two, three, and sometimes more of a side.—In those days a French nobleman was making up his party to decide a quarrel with another person of equal rank; it came to the King's ears, who sent to him one of the most rising men at court with a command to desist, assuring him of the strict execution of the edict in case of disobedience.—Every one knows the attachment the French once had to their sovereign, but yet it proved weak when set against this all-powerful passion. The nobleman not only refused to obey the King, but actually

tually

tually engaged the meffenger to be one
of his party.

The above feem to be the principal
reafons why riches, cards, and duelling
have fo deep a root in the mind of man
—but there are others which come in aid.
The defire of fuperiority is of itfelf almoft fufficient to produce this great effect.

Believe me ever yours, &c.

LETTER

LETTER III.

I Cannot comply with your defire—a regular differtation is above me—but if you will take my thoughts as they occur, the honour of methodizing them fhall be yours.

Languages are termed rough and fmooth, weak or expreffive, frequently without reafon.—As thefe are comparative terms, they change their application according to circumftances. The French is faid to be a fmooth or rough language, when compared with the German or Italian. Perhaps this is true; and yet we fhould not determine too haftily. In appearance there are more vowels in the Italian language than in the French: but in pronunciation the French lofe many confonants,

fonants, and the Italians none : yet in
French, from irregularities incident to
all languages, there is fometimes an effect
of confonants pronounced, which are not
written—fmoothnefs or roughnefs muft
therefore depend on the ear alone; yet
how far a language is weak or expreffive,
may be treated of and determined with
precifion.

Every fentence may be confidered as
the picture of an idea; the quicker that
picture is prefented to the mind, the
ftronger is its impreffion. That language then which is fhorteft, is the moft
expreffive. If we fhould fix on any language as being in general the moft con-
cife, yet, if in fome inftances it is more
diffufe than another, then, in thofe inftances the latter is moft expreffive.
This, I believe, is an univerfal rule, and
without exception.

. Let .

Let us for the prefent fuppofe Latin to be' more expreffive, becaufe fhorter, than any modern language, and compare it with Englifh in fome examples, juft as they occur. *Captus oculis* and *cæcus* are ufed for the fame thing—the laft is more expreffive than the firft, and both lefs fo than *blind:* a fingle fyllable does the office of many. How much more forcibly does it ftrike us to be told that our friend is dead, than *mortuus eft*, or *Mors continuo ipfum occupavit?* This laft is indeed poetical, if we fuppofe death a perfon.

Tranflations, are ufually more verbofe than their original, which is one reafon for their weaknefs; whenever they are lefs fo, they are ftronger. Suppofe we fhould find in a French author thefe phrafes, *Un Canon de neuf livres de Balle* —*Un Vaiffeau du Roi du quatre vingt dix Pieces du Canon;* and they were rendered into Englifh by a *nine-pounder*—*A ninety-gun fhip*—is not the tranflation more fpirited

rited than the original ? I purpofely chofe a phrafe with as little matter in it as pof-fible, where the meaning could not be miftaken, and in which there was no variety of expreffion, that the trial might be fairer.

Although I juft now faid that Latin was clofer in its expreffion than any mo-dern language, it was only in compli-ance with common opinion ; for there is fome reafon to believe that it yields in this refpect to Englifh : the Latin hexa-meter and Terence's line being with eafe included in our heroic verfe, which is not fo long by many fyllables. Many pieces of Englifh poetry have been tranf-lated into Latin, and, when compared with the original, nothing can read more dead and inanimated. To fave the trou-ble of referring to examples, I fhall give an inftance from one of the beft poets of

C   the

the age, which is more to the purpofe
as the tranflation is his own.

> The nymph muft lofe her female friend.
>   If more admir'd than fhe ;
> But where will fierce contention end,
>   If flow'rs can difagree ?

> Heu inimicitias quoties parit æmula forma !
>   Quam raro pulchræ, pulchra placere poteft ?
> Sed fines ultrà folitos difcordia tendit
>   Cum flores ipfos bilis et ira movent.

Take another example from the fame
ingenious author—it is a tranflation of
Prior's Chloe and Euphelia,

> The merchant, to fecure his treafure,
>   Conveys it in a borrow'd name ;
> Euphelia ferves to grace my meafure,
>   But Chloe is my real flame.

> Mercator, vigiles oculos ut fallere poffit,
>   Nomine fub fi&to trans mare mittit opes ;
> Lenè fonat liquidumque meis Euphelia chordis,
>   Sed folam exoptant te, mea vota, Chlöe.

Obferve, how the fame thought is
strong

ftrong in Englifh and weak in Latin, occafioned entirely by its being clofe in one
language, and diffufe in the other: for
as much as a fentence exceeds another in
length, in the fame proportion does it
fail in expreffion.

I have heard that the German is an expreffive language—I do not underftand
it; but I can perceive that, for the moft
part, the words are very long, which
makes againft its being fo. French and
Italian particularly, are generally more
diffufe than Englifh. Tranflations from
thefe languages have often a force that
the originals wanted; and this not owing
to the Englifh being a ftronger language
in *found*, as fome have fuppofed, for the
Italian is the moft fonorous of any, but
to ftrength occafioned by brevity.

It has been obferved, that there is no
language which fo abounds in monofyl-
lables as the Englifh; and this is generally mentioned as a defect; but, if the

fore-

foregoing remarks be true, it is rather an excellence. Thofe writers who affeét the verba fefquipedalia, lofe more by delaying to prefent the idea to the mind, than they gain by filling the mouth with pompous fyllables,

The three languages of Europe in which moft works of imagination and tafte are written, have, when compared with the others, the fhorteft words and fentences. On the contrary, fome favage tongues have more fyllables to exprefs the number *one*, than we ufe to get as far as *ten*. May we not from hence conclude, that brevity is one charaéteriftic of a cultivated language?

Perhaps it may be imagined, that thofe words which carry their fignification with them fhould be moft expreffive, whether long or fhort; that is, when they are derived from, or compounded of known words, which exprefs that fignification.

I   But

But this is not fo. When we fay, *adieu*, *farewell*—we mean no more than a cere-mony at parting.—No one confiders *adieu* * as a recommendation to God, or *farewell* as a wifh for happinefs.--Frequent ufe deftroys all idea of derivation. But if we fpeak a compound or felf-fignificative word that is not common, we perceive the derivation of it. Thus if a Lon-doner fays *butter milk*, he has the idea of fomething compounded of *butter* and *milk;* but to an Irifhman or Hollander, it is as fimple an idea as either of the words taken feparately, is to us.

It is but of late that our orthography was fixed, even in the moft common words. Two hundred years ago, every perfon fpelt as he liked, a privilege en-joyed ftill later than that period by "royal

* " Prononce *Amen*, donne ton ame *à Dieu*— '
Non, répondit le maraud à tonfure,
Je fuis damné, je vais au diable, *adieu!*"

and noble authors," who feem, in this
inftance, to claim the liberty enjoyed by
their anceftors.* Since the time orthography has been thought of fome confequence, we have attended partly to pronunciation, tho' chiefly to derivation.
But, in fome cafes, where we fhould altogether have fpelt according to derivation, we have taken pronunciation for our
guide. And this has occafioned fome
confufion ; for inftance *naught* is *bad—*
nought is *nothing ;* thefe terms were long
confounded, and even now are not kept
perfectly diftinct, which has occafioned
ought to be written *aught*. *Wrapt* is en-
velloped—*rapt* is hurried away, or totally poffeffed : the firft of thefe has been
ufed for the laft, by one of the correcteft
of our modern poets.† *Marry* is an af-

* This was written juft after the publication of a
correfpondence which gave ample occafion for the
remark.

† " Since wrapt Mufæus tun'd his parting lay. "

feveration

feveration—*marry*, to give in marriage—
the fpelling thefe words the fame, confounds them together; we fhould have
preferved for the firft, the real word *mary*.
It was a common thing formerly to fwear
by *Mary*, the *a* in which was pronounced
broad, as the Priefts of that time did the
Latin *Maria*, from whom the common
people took the pronunciation. In one of
the pieces in the firft volume of the collection of old plays, it frequently occurs,
and is fpelt as a proper name, *Marie*.
Permit me to obferve, that the editor, by
modernizing the fpelling in the other vo-
lumes, has prevented their being made
this ufe of, as they might have fhewed
the progrefs of orthography as well as of
dramatic poetry.

In the reign of James the firft were many
attempts to reduce orthography altogether
to pronunciation. In our time we have
feen fome attempts to bring it altogether
from derivation—but furely both were
wrong.

wrong. .Whoever reads Howel's letters, or Dr. Newton's Milton, will fee, that by a partial principle too generally adopted, they have made of the Englifh language " a very fantaftical banquet—juft fo many ftrange difhes !"

There are many inverfions of phrafes ufed in poetry which are contrary to the genius of our language. In Pope's tranf- lation of the Iliad there frequently occurs " thunders the fky,"——" totters the ground," meaning that " the fky thun- ders," and " the ground totters." This change of pofition has the authority of fome of our beft poets, tho' it frequently obfcures the fenfe, and fometimes makes it directly contrary to what is intended to be expreffed. Our language does not, with eafe, admit of the nominative, after the verb. If we read, tho' in poetry, " fhakes the ground," we do not rea- dily underftand that " the ground fhakes," but rather refer to fome antecedent nomi- native that has produced this effect. To adopt

adopt the conftruction of the ancient languages is as awkward as to adopt their
meafures. You will underftand this to
be meant as a general obfervation, the
truth of which is not deftroyed by a few
exceptions where the inverfion may be
happily ufed. The fenfe in thefe verfes
of Pope " halts" as much by Roman
conftruction, as the Rhythmus in Sydney
does by " Roman feet.*"

In reading Latin and Greek we are obliged to keep the fenfe fufpended until
we come to the end of the period, but it
is not fo in any modern tongue with
which I am acquainted, except now and
then in Italian poetry ; fo that there is a
famenefs of conftruction in all of them
when compared with the ancient languages. Now, this fufpenfion of the
fenfe is furely no advantage ; therefore if

* " And Sydney's verfe halts ill on Roman feet."

it

it were poffible to make Englifh like Latin and Greek in this refpect, it would hurt the language.

In another letter I may poffibly refume this fubject, which is capable of much curious difquifition.

I am, &c.

LETTER

LETTER IV.

OUR greateſt miſtake in the purſuit of happineſs as well as of ſcience, is to judge by the perceptions of others, and not by our own. This perverſion is admirably ridiculed in ſome comedy, in which a young fellow naturally ſober, gives into debaucheries merely becauſe they are faſhionable. "I am horrid ſick"—ſays he—" I am tired to death— I hate cards—but it is *life* for all that!"

This word, if one could know the truth, has probably occaſioned much more pain than pleaſure. There are ſo few who are qualified to undergo the fatigue of diſſipation, that our places of public reſort are moſtly filled by thoſe who only go becauſe it is the faſhion.

At

At a mafquerade where a thoufand perfons affemble in order to be happy, it
would be difficult to felect fifty that have
a real enjoyment of it—the reft go, becaufe it is *life*. How few who walk the
" never-ending, ftill-beginning" round
of Ranelagh, but with longing eyes pafs
the door, and envy thofe who have refo-
lution to make their exit ?

The tax we pay to imitation is not
levied in town only—it is full as high in
the country, and paid with as much re-
luctance. But we are in all cafes afhamed
to obey the pathetic remonftrances of our
honeft feelings. Although they tell us
that the pleafure of fhooting is not equal
to the pains, we do not quit the gun.
Although the mufic of the dogs has not
a charm fufficient to remove the fear of
breaking one's neck, yet we gallop on.
And although the " *im*patient fifher"
ftill holds his rod extended, he longs to
shorten

fhorten it into a walking-ftick, jemmy,
and fwitch.

How many pretend to receive pleafure
from pictures who have no eye—to feel
raptures at mufic, that have no ear—and
to be tranfported with the charms of
poetry, tho', like Falftaff's recruits, they
are preffed into the fervice " with hearts
no bigger than pin's heads ? "

" It is *tafte*—it is *life* to do this"—
but it is not *your* tafte—however, all
matters may be eafily adjufted—here—

—————hinc Vos,
Vos hinc, mutatis difcedite partibus—

Now confefs honeftly, Mr. Sportfman,
that you have more pleafure in Snyder's
pictures, than from hunting in propriâ
perfonâ—that the French horns at a concert have more harmony than in a wood.
And, Mr. Connoiffeur, you are now in
your element.—Is it not better to " join
the

the jovial chace" than the infipid crew
of the dilettanti ?

Let us remember and practice the old
maxim.

———trahit *fua* quemque Voluptas.

LETTER

LETTER V.

Dear Sir,

I AM glad you go on with your painting. Though you fhould never arrive at any great degree of excellence yourfelf, it will infallibly make you a better judge of the excellencies of others. You tell me, what indeed every Connoiffeur fays by rote, that the great painters painted above, beyond nature! That they painted beyond nature I grant, but not above, if by above we are to underftand fomething more excellent than what we find in nature. I have long been fick of the cant of writers and talkers upon this fubject. If it be poffible, let us fpeak a little common-fenfe—endeavour to fhew what feems by our feelings to be the

truth,

truth, and then prevent a wrong application of it.

The great painters, it is agreed, painted beyond nature—but how? Why, if I
may venture to fay it, by drawing and
colouring extravagantly. But were they
right or wrong in doing fo? This de-
pends upon circumftances. I remember
feeing at a Painter's a head taken from
nature, another copied from Hans Holbein, and a third from Giulio Romano—
upon which the artift made a differtation.—He firft produced the portrait
from nature, and afked me how I liked
it? I told him that there appeared to me
great fimplicity and elegance in it, and
an excellence which I thought effential to
a good picture—a proper balance between
the light and fhade of every part. (I
meant that the fhade of the white was
lighter than that of blue—of blue fain-
ter than that of black, &c. fo that each
colour was as perceivable in the fhadows
as lights.) Ay, fays he, that is true,
but

but I will fhew you a ftyle preferable to it—Upon which he produced the copy from Holbein.—I agreed, that it was ftronger, and fuch as nature might appear in many inftances.—But here, fays he, is fomething *beyond* nature; this I call the fublime ftyle of painting, and this I will try to bring my heads to.—Then he difcovered the copy from Giulio—there is ftrength, fays he—fee how faint the others are.—Now, acknowledge that the picture I painted from nature is nothing to it. It muft be confeffed, I replied, that the extravagance of the laft picture does for a moment dazzle our eyes—yours feem weak by the comparifon; it is looking upon white paper after ftaring at the fun.—On the contrary, if I pafs from yours to this, I am hurt at feeing every thing fo extravagant, and fo far *beyond the modefty of nature!*——" It is not intended to be ftrictly natural, it is the *fine ideal*; it is fomething above, beyond nature!"

D

I muft

I muft own that I have no idea of any beauty beyond what may be found in na- ture—indeed, whence is the idea to be taken? But do not think I rate Giulio or any of the fublime painters lightly; I am fo fenfible of their merit, that, contrary perhaps to your expectation, I am about to defend their practice. They generally painted for churches, where the picture is feen in a bad light, or at a dif- tance; fo that it could not be feen at all if the manner was not violent: both the drawing and colouring muft be extrava- gant to ftrike—for which reafon, they overcharged their attitudes, blackened their fhadows, reddened their carnations, and whitened their lights; and all this with the greateft propriety. But if you apply this practice to clofet or portrait painting, what is an excellence in them, becomes a defect in you. This picture which you have copied with fo much fuccefs, I dare fay has an admirable ef- fect where it hangs; but near the eye or

in

in a ftrong light, it is hard and over-
done. On the other hand, if your portrait was to be hung at a great diftance,
or in an obfcure place, the delicate touches
I now admire would efcape the fight.
The ftyle proper for the church is improper for the clofet, and the contrary.
The great painters were in the right then,
in painting *beyond nature;* but let us not
imagine that fuch figures and characters
are therefore the moft beautiful. No
painter can invent a figure furpaffing the
fineft of nature : for character and form,
nature is the *juft* and *only* ftandard. He
fhews his genius more by properly affo-
ciating natural objects, and expreffing
natural characters, than by exaggerating
them or by inventing new ones.

This muft not be underftood as object-
ing to painters defign'ng from ideas of
general nature. Hiftorical pictures which
have fome antient ftory for their fubject,
can only be fo expreffed : for if the fea-

tures,

tures, air, or drefs were like what we
daily fee, the effect is deftroyed, and the
picture lofes in dignity and confequence.
Thofe circumftances of which we can
have no precife idea, fhould be exprefled
generally, and fomething left to be fupplied by the imagination, which always
does much more for the artift, than he
can poffibly do for himfelf.

We are fo ufed to expect *general* nature, that we do not foon relifh hiftorical pictures on modern fubjects, becaufe
they cannot be painted upon that principle. Perhaps this kind of painting
ought to be allowed principles of its
own, and conftitute a feparate branch of
the art.

It is not much difconnected from this
fubject, to remark the miftake of thofe
artifts who in their defigns for plays, inftead of exhibiting the character, give a
portrait of the actor reprefenting it.
Gravelot

Gravelot (in Theobald's Shakefpeare)
knew the impropriety of this and avoided it.

When I receive the picture you have
promifed me, I will criticife it with as
much fincerity as

I am your Friend, &c.

LETTER

LETTER VI.

YOU have turned my thoughts much towards painting of late—I have been trying to folve this queftion.

What is the reafon that thofe objects which difpleafe us, or at beft, that pafs unnoticed, in nature, pleafe us moft in painting?

A deep road, a puddle of water, a bank covered with docks and briars, and an old tree or two, are all the circumftan-ces in many a fine landfcape. As clowns and half-ftarved cattle are the figures a landfcape painter chufes for his pictures; fo rough-looking fellows wrapt up in fheets and blankets, are chofen by the hiftory-painter, to exprefs the greateft

per-

perfonages, and in the moft dignified actions of their lives.

Let the following obfervations have what weight they may—tho' they do not clearly anfwer, they feem to throw fome light on this difficult queftion.

1. While we are uncultivated, like the Irifh Ofcar, if we are to be awakened, it muft be by having a great ftone thrown againft our heads. The man of the utmoft elegance and refinement may remember the time when, in reading, nothing moved him but the marvellous; and in painting, nothing pleafed him but the glaring. While he was in this ftate, he delighted in books of chivalry and Chinefe pictures—thefe gave place to lefs extravagant reprefentations of life; and at laft by much converfe with men of tafte, reading purer authors, and feeing better pictures, he is taught how to feel, and finds a perfect revolution even in his

2   fenfa-

fenfations. Thofe objects which once delighted him, he now defpifes—others, on the contrary, he formerly took no notice of, he now fees with rapture; and even goes fo far as to be pleafed with the objects in nature, *he has learnt* to like in reprefentation.—Now, it is this improved, tho' artificial, ftate of the mind that conftitutes the judge of paint-ing—and it is the judge the painter is folicitous to pleafe.—He is to attain this end then, by departing as much as poffi-ble from what is our natural barbarous tafte, and by conforming to that we have acquired.

2. It is moft certain, that in all the arts we make difficulties in order to fhew our fkill in conquering them.—Some French writer calls this principle *la diffi-culté vaincue*; and this conqueft is the fource of much pleafure. What is it but this, that induces the novelift and play-writer to embarrafs their characters with

with difficulties and troubles? What is
there but this, that can induce a mufician
to beftow fo much pains to compofe a
canon? and, to bring it to the prefent
fubject—what is it but this, that induces
the painter to make ufe of the moft un-
promifing objects, and produce beauty
from the very circumftances that feem to
promife nothing but difguft and defor-
mity?

3. It is neceffary that a painter fhould
chufe fuch objects as are capable of variety either from fhape or arrangement.
Regular formal objects admit but little,
efpecially thofe where art has the greateft
fhare in their production; unlefs they are
capable of motion, as fhips, windmills,
&c. and then they become pictorefque
by a proper choice of attitude. It is
curious to obferve the fhifts to which
artifts are reduced, when they are obliged
to paint fuch objects as are in themfelves
unpictorefque—fuppofe a fine houfe with

avenues

avenues of trees. They will vary the tint of the ftones in the one, and of the leaves in the other, or by throwing in accidental fhades and lights produce a variety. In like manner, portrait-painters undrefs the hair, loofen the coat, and wrinkle the ftockings that they may produce a variety in the *manner* of *treating* a fubject which was wanting in its form.

Thofe objects which have no fet form have of courfe moft variety. A road, or river may wind in any direction— trees are of all fizes and fhapes, may ftand here or there—loofe drapery admits a thoufand folds and difpofitions of which the ftiff modern drefs is incapable. So that the painter by taking thefe, has ample materials for fhewing his judgment in form, or fkill in arrangement— for making, and overcoming difficulties —and laftly, by the uniting both thefe, he conforms to the principles by which

the

the cultivated tafte is pleafed—the ultimate end of all the fine arts.

If you are not fatisfied with this folution, help me to a better—but give a fair reading to this of

Your fincere friend, &c.

LETTER

I Do not admit your excufe.—A genius fhould never comply with *local* or *temporary* tafte—inftead of debafing himfelf to the people, he fhould elevate the people to him. When Milton fubtilizes divinity, and Shakefpeare " cracks the wind of a poor phrafe ;" who but wifhes that thofe great poets had not defcended from their fphere ?

Your allufions to incidents which muft foon be forgotten, are only worthy of a writer who expects but a fhort exiftence. It is true our plays abound with fuch allufions. When Foigard, in the Beaux Stratagem, fays he is a fubject to the King of Spain——they afk him in a fury, " which King of Spain ?" This did very well

well at the time; but thefe two Kings of
Spain are now of much lefs confequence
than their brother monarchs of Brentford.
I think it is in the fame play where one of
the characters is afked " when he was at
church laft?" he fhould anfwer, " at the
coronation;" but it is a point to give a
reply that fhall fuit the time when
the play is performed, and it is either
inftallation or coronation, according
to prefent circumftances, forgetting
that there are many expreffions which
fet you back into the laft century when
the play was written.

Nothing feems fairer ground in a comedy than fatirical allufions to the drefs
in fafhion where it lies open to remark or
ridicule; and yet, this is of fo tranfitory
a nature, that when the mode changes,
the wit vanifhes. There are many paffages in Cibbers's plays, and in others of
the fame age, that owe all their fmartnefs
to the character being dreffed in a full-
bottomed

bottomed flaxen periwig. When the farce of Lethe firſt made its appearance, dreſſed hair and a queue were confidered as marks of a coxcomb.—Says Æfop, " let me advife you to lay afide your *wings* and your *tail* for they undoubtedly eclipfe your manhood"—this has now loſt its fatire.

However, the local and temporary wit which we diflike in the play, we applaud in the prologue or epilogue, where it is in its proper place.

In writing, as in painting, all produc- tions of the higher clafs muſt fcorn to de- pend upon any particular country or age for their propriety. The characters of Lear or Falſtaffe, tho' as great contraſts as can be found in the whole range of human na- ture, are both formed upon general prin- ciples, fo that they are equally excellent now, as when they were firſt exhibited, and they will produce the utmoſt effect of tragedy

tragedy and comedy as long as our language endures. This would not be the cafe if either were the portrait of an individual; like other portraits they would appear uninterefting, and even ridiculous, when their drefs ceafed to be that of the prefent day.

Local, and temporary allufions then, not only lofe their intended effect, but produce a bad one, as foon as the circumftances vanifh to which they owe their original.

Adieu, &c.

LETTER

LETTER VIII.

TRUE, my friend, muficians do commit ftrange abfurdities by way of expreffion—but fanciful people make them
commit others which they never thought
of.

The moft common miftake of compofers is to exprefs words and not ideas.
This is generally the cafe with Purcel,
and frequently the cafe with Handel. I
believe there is not a fingle piece exifting
of the former, if it has a word to be
played upon, but will prove my affertion :
and the latter, if the impetuofity of the
mufical fubject will give him leave, will
at any time quit it for a pun. There is
no trap fo likely to catch compofers as
the

the words *high* and *low*, *down* and *up*.
" By G— (as Quin fays) they muft
bite." In what raptures was Purcel when
he fet " They that *go down* to the fea in
fhips." How lucky a circumftance, that
there was a finger at that time, who could
go down to DD, and *go up* two octaves
above? for there is in other parts of the
anthem a going *up* as well as *down*. The
whole is a conftellation of be uties of
this kind. Handel had leifure, at the
conclufion of an excellent movement, to
endeavour at an imitation of the rocking
of a cradle. (See the end of the anthem
" My heart is inditing,") and has his
ups and *downs* too in plenty. If many
examples of this may be found in thefe
great geniufes, it would be endlefs to enu-
merate the inftances of thofe of the lower
order. Let it fuffice to obferve, that all
operas without exception, the greateft
part of church-mufic, and particularly
Marcello's pfalms, abound in this ridiculous imitative expreffion.

E   This

· This is trifling with the words and neglecting the fentiment ; but the fault is much increafed when a word is expreffed in contradiction to the fentiment. A moft flagrant inftance of this is in Boyce's Solomon, in the fong of " Arife, my Fairone, come away."—The hero of the piece is inviting his miftrefs to come to him, and to tempt her the more, in defcribing the beauty of the fpring, he tells her that

" Stern winter's *gone*, with all its train
" Of chilling frofts and dropping rain."

but it is *come*, in the mufic—the unlucky words of *winter*, *froft*, and *rain*, made the compofer fet the lover a fhivering, when he was full of the feelings of the " genial ray !"

But fometimes expreffion of the fentiment is blameable, if fuch expreffion is improper for the general effect of the piece. Religious folemnity fhould not appear at the

the theatre, nor theatrical levity at the
church. In the *Stabat Mater* of Pergo-
lefi, and in the *Meſſiah* of Handel, there
is an expreſſion of whipping attempted,
which, if it be underſtood at all, con-
veys either a ludicrous or prophane idea,
according to the difpofition of the hearer.
Permit me to fufpend my remarks a mo-
ment, juft to obferve, that there is fometimes mention made in plays, of Provi-
dence, God, and other fubjects, which
are as incompatible with a place of public entertainment, as the common fentiments of plays are with the church. If
we are difgufted at a theatrical preacher,
we are not lefs offended when an actor
heightens all thefe ill-placed fentiments—
forcing them upon your notice by an affectation of a deep fenfe of religion, and
moft folemnly preaching the fermon
which the poet fo improperly wrote.

All thefe, and many more, are faults
which muficians *really* commit; but a

.con-

connoiffeur will make them guilty of others, by way of compliment, which the compofers never dreamt of. The introduction of the coronation anthem, *Zadok the Prieft*, is an arpeggio, which Handel probably took from his own performance at the harpfichord ; but a great judge fays, it is to exprefs the murmurs of the people affembled in the abbey. " *All we like fheep are gone aftray*" in the Meffiah, is confidered as moft excellently expreffing the breaking out of fheep from a field. But out of pity to the connoiffeurs, I will not increafe my inftances— God forbid I fhould rob any man of his criticifm.

Left I fhould encroach upon *your* premifes, I will quit fuch dangerous ground, and leave you with more celerity than ceremony.

LETTER

LETTER IX.

I APPROVE every part of your poem except the parenthefis towards the con-clufion. In the midft of a rapid de-fcription, or tender fentiment; or any thing that commands the attention, or attaches the heart; what is more difguft-ful than to have the image cut in two, for the fake of explaining a word, or re-moving an objection, which the reader may poffibly make?

Milton and Shakefpeare frequently in-terrupt the moft lively and ardent paf-fages—take fome inftances as they occur.

Their arms away they threw, and to the hills
(For earth hath this variety from heav'n
Of pleafure fituate in hill or dale)
Light as the lightning's glimpfe they ran, they flew.

PAR. LOST, B. VI.

—————when

————————when on a day
(For time, though in eternity, apply'd
To motion, meafures all things durable
By prefent, paft, and future) on fuch a day
As heaven's great year brings forth.

PAR. LOST, B. V.

————————evening now approach'd,
(For we have alfo our evening and our morn,
We ours for change delectable, not need)
Forthwith from dance to fweet repaft they turn
Defirous; &c.

Upon the mention of *hills* in the firft quotation, and of *day* and *evening* in the fecond and laft—he knew that he had fome objections to anfwer, and accordingly fet about doing it for fear of the confequences—I wifh they had remained in their full force.

Milton's general ftyle in the Paradife Loft is fo full of fhort parenthefes, that the fenfe is perplexed, and the grandeur of the idea frequently deftroyed. Thefe are not marked nor pointed as fuch, which occafions a difficulty in the con-

ftruc-

ſtruction, and an interruption in the flow
of the verſe, reducing it to mere proſe,
and almoſt juſtifying the ſevere cenſures
of a late critic.

You have often read the Midſummer
Night's Dream—do you recollect this
paſſage?

Lyſ. Hermia, for ought that ever I could read,
Could ever hear by tale or hiſtory,
The courſe of true love never did run ſmooth;
But, either it was different in blood—.—
 Her. O croſs! too high, to be enthrall'd to low!——
 Lyſ. Or elſe miſgrafted in reſpect of years—
 Her. O ſpite! too old, to be engag'd to young!
 Lyſ. Or elſe it ſtood upon the choice of friends—
 Her. O hell! to chuſe love by another's eye!
 Lyſ. Or if there were a ſympathy in choice—
War, death, or ſickneſs did lay ſiege to it.

With theſe interruptions the effect is entirely loſt—without them, it becomes
one of the fineſt paſſages in Shakeſpeare.

You will remember that it is the improper uſe of the parentheſis I object to,
          and

and not to the thing itfelf. " This figure of compofition, fays a late ingenious author, which is hardly ever ufed in
common difcourfe, is much employed by
the beft writers of antiquity, in order to
give a caft and colour to their ftyle different from common idiom,. and by De-
mofthenes particularly; and not only by
the orators, but the poets."

I would recommend to your confidera-
tion, whether you had not better avoid giving any hint how the ftory of your poem is
to conclude? Anticipation frequently
fpoils a fine incident. Æneas, reciting
to Dido what paffed at Troy, fays

Arduus armatos mediis in mænibus aftans
Fundit equus.
                                        Æn. II.

The firft mention of the Horfe's having armed men within, fhould have been
referved for this place. There is fomething

thing truly terrible and fublime in
Æneas being waked by fuch a variety
of horrid founds, and ignorant of the
caufe; the reader alfo fhould have been
ignorant until Pantheus explained the
myftery. See the whole paffage in Æn.
II. beginning at the 298th verfe, and if
poffible, forget that this went before :

> Delecta virum fortiti corpora furtim
> Includunt cæco lateri, &c.

One of the fineft parts of Don Quixote is alfo fpoiled by mentioning a circumftance which fhould have been de-
layed. The Knight and his 'Squire, at
the clofe of the day, hear the clank of
chains, and dreadful blows, which would
have puzzled the reader as much as it
frightened them, had not the author un-
luckily faid, " that the ftrokes were in
time and *meafure*," which is telling us
very plainly that it was a mill. The
whole fcene is highly pictorefque and
beautiful.

As

As the effect of a paſſage is ſpoiled by anticipation, ſo is it by protraction—by being continued after the thought and expreſſion are finiſhed. Thus when the Ghoſt of Ajax turns indignant from Ulyſſes, not deigning a reply, it is a noble inſtance of the ſublime in character *;

and

* Moſt of theſe *ſilences* are mere affectation. " Were ever ſorrow, and miſery, and compaſſion, (I abridge the paſſage from The Adventurer) more forcibly expreſſed than by Job's friends who ſat down with him ſeven nights? &c. Let us confeſs that this is ſuperior to the deſcription of parental ſorrow in Æſchylus, who has repreſented Niobe ſitting three days upon the tomb of her children, &c. Such ſilences are more affecting and expreſſive of paſſion than the moſt artful ſpeeches. In Sophocles, when Dejanira diſcovers her miſtake in ſending the poiſoned veſtment to Hercules, her ſurprize and ſorrow are unſpeakable, and ſhe goes off the ſtage without uttering a ſyllable, &c."

Perhaps, in *nature*, if a father informed of the ſudden death of a beloved ſon, was to ſay nothing, the ſilence would be more affecting than any reply, but it certainly has not the ſame effect on the ſtage.

There

and here, to produce effect, should have
been the conclusion of the incident. But
when Ulyſſes adds, that tho' Ajax was ſo
angry, he would have tried to make him
ſpeak, if he had not wiſhed to ſee ſome
other ghoſts; the ſenſation is ſo much
abaſed, that we accuſe Ulyſſes of wanting heroic feeling, and almoſt fancy that
the poet himſelf was not ſenſible of his
own ſublimity.

No writer knew ſo well when, and how,
to finiſh a paſſage as Voltaire. The ma-

There, it ſeems, not as if grief had taken away the
power of utterance, but that the poet was deficient
in invention. The tragedy of Agis has a circumſtance of this ſort, but it was ſo far from producing
the effect intended, that the audience conſidered it as
a poor triek, and had " great diſpoſitions to laugh."
Job's friends ſitting down with him in ſilence, as a
relation of ſomething that had happened, is affecting;
but, repreſent it on the ſtage, and it becomes ridiculous. I do not ſee the ſublimity of ſitting ſilent for
ſeven days together. If this long, *impoſſible;* time is
ſublime, then it would be more ſublime if the ſeven
days had been fourteen—but we are never taken in
by ſuch things.

gic

gic of his ftyle, in great meafure, de-
pends upon his attention to this principle. Every fentence has. fomething in
the turn of it which marks a termination—a paragraph more particularly fo;
and a chapter, or book, are moft ftrongly
marked of all.

There. are inftances of an abrupt termination producing a bad effect. The
Æneid certainly wants a finifh—there is
too much left to be fuppofed—we may
fay this, without approving of a thir-
teenth book added by another poet. The
moft complete cataftrophe of a ftory is
that of Tom Jones, which is the beft
invented, the beft conducted, and the
beft finifhed fable that the wit of man
has yet produced.

If thefe hints will be of any fervice to
you, it will be a great pleafure to

Yours, &c.

LETTER

LETTER X.

THE productions of genius require fome ages to be brought to perfection. The liberal arts have their infancy, youth, and manhood ; and, to carry on the allufion, continue fome time in a ftate of ftrength, and then verge by degrees to a decline, which at laft ends in a total extinction. The Englifh language, poetry, and mufic, exhibit proofs of this obfervation, as far as they have hitherto gone : with the two former I have at prefent nothing to do, but fhall confine what I have to fay on this fubject, to the latter.

What the mufic of the times preceding Harry the eighth was, I confefs myfelf ignorant, nor indeed is the knowledge of

it

it neceffary.; we may conclude that it was more barbarous than that of the fixteenth century, as the times in which it was ufed were lefs enlightened. Some maffes, mottets, and madrigals are what have reached us, confifting merely in a fucceffion of chords without art or meaning, and perfectly deftitute of air.

In Elizabeth's reign appeared fome compofers, Tallis, Bird, Morley, and Farrant, who improved the barren ftyle of their predeceffors: they had more choice in their harmony, and made fome little advances in melody. There were fome pieces of inftrumental mufic compofed at this time which ftill exift: par-. ticularly a book of leffons, for the virginals, which was the Queen's.—Whether the compofers thought that her facred Majefty excelled in mufical abilities as much as in rank, or as fhe wifhed to do in beauty, I know not; but this is certain, that thefe pieces are fo crowded with

with parts, and fo awkwardly barbarous,
as to render the performance of them impoffible—fo natural is it, even in the infancy of art, to miftake difficulty for
beauty.

I do not recollect any compofer that
really improved mufic for the firft half of
the feventeenth century, except Orlando
Gibbons; of whom a fervice for the
church, and two or three anthems remain, the harmony of which is good,
and the melody, for the times, pleafing.
In the Gloria Patri of the Nunc Dimittis
is the beft canon, in my judgment, that
was ever made. Gibbons was alfo a compofer for the virginals, but in no refpect
better than his predeceffors. I believe it
was about this time that the fpecies of
canon called the catch, was produced.
The intent of my making this fhort re-
capitulation of the former ftate of mufic,
is purely prefatory to what I have to fay
upon the fubject of catches.

This

This odd fpecies of compofition, whenever invented, was brought to its perfection by Purcel. Real mufic was as yet in
its childhood ; but the reign of Charles
the fecond carried every kind of vulgar
debauchery to its height : the proper æra
for the birth of fuch pieces as " when
quartered, have ever three parts obfce-
nity, and one part mufic."

The definition of a catch is a piece for
three or more voices, one of which leads,
and the others follow in the fame notes.
It muſt be fo contrived, that reſts (which
are made for that purpofe) in the mufic
of one line, be filled up with a word or
two from another line; thefe form a
crofs-purpofe or catch, from whence the
name. Now, this piece of wit is not
judged perfect, if the refult be not the
rankeſt indecency.

Perhaps this definition may be objected
to, and I may be told that there are
catches

catches perfectly harmlefs. It is true that fome pieces are called catches that have nothing to offend, and others that may juftly pretend to pleafe; but they want what is abfolutely neceffary for a catch— the break, and crofs-purpofe.

It may alfo be faid, that the refult of the break is not always indecency. I con- fefs, there are catches upon other fubjects: drunkennefs is a favourite one; which, though good, is not fo *very* good as the other: and there may poffibly be found one or two upon other topicks, which might be heard without difguft; but thefe are not fufficient to contradict a general rule, or make me retract what I have ad- vanced.

I will next examine their mufical me- rit.—And this, as compofitions, muft confift either in their harmony, or me- lody; or their effect in performance.

F   The

The harmony of a catch is nothing
more than the common refult of filling
up a chord.—There is not contrivance
enough to make it efteemed as a piece of
ingenuity. " What ! they are all ca-
nons !" So is every tune in the world, if
you will fet it in three or more parts, and
fing thefe parts in fucceffion, as a catch—
but a *real* canon is not fo eafily produced:
it is one of thofe difficult trifles which
cofts an infinite deal of labour, and after
all is worth nothing. The excellence in
the compofition of a catch confifts in
making the breaks, and filling them up
properly. The melody, is, for the moft
part, the unimproved vulgar drawl of the
times of ignorance.

Let us next attend to the manner of
performance. One voice leads, a fecond
follows, and a third, &c. fucceeds, un-
accompanied with any inftrument to keep
them in tune together. The confequence
is, that the voices are always finking;
but

but not equally, for the beſt ſinger will keep neareſt the pitch, and the others depart fartheſt from it. If the parts are doubled, which is ſometimes the caſe, all theſe defects are multiplied. To this, let there be added the imperfect ſcale of an uncultivated voice, the *departing* from the real ſound by ẅay of humour, the noiſe of ſo many people ſtriving to out-ſing each other, the confuſion of ſpeaking different words at the ſame time, and all this heightened by the laughing and other accompaniments of the audience—it preſents ſuch a ſcene of ſavage folly, as would not diſgrace the Hottentots indeed, but is not much to the credit of a company of civilized people.

As the catch in a manner owed its exiſtence to a drunken club, of which ſome muſicians were members; upon their dying, it languiſhed for years, and was ſcarce known except among choir-men, who now and then kept up the ſpirit of

their

their forefathers. As the age grew more
polifhed, a better ftyle of mufic appeared.
Corelli gave a new turn to inftrumental
mufic, and was fuccefsfully followed by
Geminiani and Handel; the laft excellent
in vocal as well as inftrumental mufic.

There have been refinements and confeffed improvements upon all thefe great
men fince; and at this time there are much
better performers, and certainly more
elegant, though perhaps lefs folid compofers.

Now, if this were fpeculation only,
is it credible that tafte fhould revert to
barbarifm? Its natural death is, to be frit-
tered away in falfe refinement; and yet,
contrary to experience in every other inftance, we have gone back a century, and
catches flourifh in the reign of George the
third. There is a club compofed of fome
of the firft people in the kingdom, who
meet profeffedly to hear this fpecies of
compofition: they cultivate it and encourage

rage it with premiums. To obtain which,
many compofers, who ought to be above
fuch nonfenfe, become candidates, and
produce fuch things

—— " one knows not what to call,
" Their generation's fo equivocal."

Sometimes a piece makes its appearance that was lately found by accident,
after a concealment of a hundred and fifty
years. When it is approved, and declared too excellent for thefe degenerate
days, the author fmiles and owns it. I
fcarce ever faw one of thefe things that
did not betray itfelf, within three bars, to
be modern. All ancient mufic has an
awkward barbarity in its firft conception
and ftructure, which, in thefe days of
refinement, it is almoft impoffible to imi-
tate, fo as to deceive a real judge of the
fubject.

I profefs that I never heard a catch fung,
but I felt more afhamed than I can exprefs,

prefs. I pretend to no more delicacy than that of the age I live in, which is very properly too refined to endure such barbarifms—I was afhamed for myfelf—for my company—and if a foreigner was prefent—for my country.

It has juft occurred to me that you like catches, and frequently help to fing them —revenge yourfelf for the liberties I have taken, by compelling me to hear fome of thefe pleafant ditties, when perhaps I may be forced to fing in my own defence.

Adieu! &c.

P. S. If you fhould have a defign to convert me—take me to the catch-club. —I confefs, and honour, the fuperior excellence of its performance, while I lament that fo noble a fubfcription fhould be lavifhed for fo poor a purpofe as keeping alive mufical falfe-wit, when it might

fo

fo powerfully fupport and encourage the
beft ftyle of compofition; and rather advance our tafte by anticipating the improvement of the coming age, than force
it back to times of barbarifm, from which
it has coft us fuch pains to emerge*.

* The fubject of this letter has been much mifun-
derftood. It is confidered as a bitter Philippic againft
finging in parts, and mufical effufions of mirth in
company. The letter itfelf, warranting no fuch
conftruction, is the only reply I fhall make to this
accufation; except remarking, that it is not the
mirth of the catch which is reproved, but its *vul-
gurity.*—Nor do the obfervations extend to thofe
pieces in parts which are *not* catches, as has been
imagined. Can it be fuppofed, that the author, who
has publifhed fo many compofitions for two, three,
and four voices, would endeavour to eftablifh principles to prevent their being performed, and make
his own works the object of his fatire?

LETTER

LETTER XI.

I Know you are one of thofe who confider our language as paft its meridian.
Some think it was in its higheft luftre in
the age of Sydney; others, in that of Addifon. Perhaps upon an impartial re-
view of it, we fhall find it more perfect
now than ever.

In the authors before the reign of Elizabeth, appears not the leaft pretence to
a fimple, natural ftyle. A man was held
unfit to write, who could not exprefs his
thoughts out of the common language;
fo that it is poffible, that their contemporaries had as much difficulty to underftand them, as ourfelves. If we are to
judge of the Englifh they fpoke, by what
they writ, we have no reafon to complain

plain of the fluctuation of our tongue.
But it is very probable that converfation-
language was much the fame two hundred
years ago as at prefent; there are proofs
of this in private letters ftill exifting—I
mean, from fuch people as had no ambition to be thought learned, or from fuch
as felt too much for affectation. The
famous letter of Anne Boleyn to Henry
the eighth, is of this laft fort, in which
there is fcarce an obfolete expreffion.—
I hope you make a diftinction between
expreffion and fpelling—for as I once
obferved to you, it is but of late that our
orthography has been fixed. In the ftate-
trials in Elizabeth and James's reign, we
find nearly the fame language that we ufe
at prefent, and this was taken immediately from the mouth. In thofe paffages
where Shakefpeare's genius had not its full
fcope, may be obferved his attempts to
be thought learned, and refined; but
where the fubject was too impetuous
to brook reftraint, the language is as
perfect

perfect as the idea. Upon the whole,
tho' the colloquial Englifh differed but
little from the prefent, we may fafely
pronounce the ftyle of the *authors* of this
period to be barbarous.

The difputes between Charles the firft
and the Parliament, were of great ufe in
polifhing the language ; and though the
King's papers are thought to be the moft
elegant, yet it is evident that both parties
endeavoured at ftrength for the good of
their caufe, and at perfpicuity for the fake
of being univerfally underftood—and
thefe two principles go near towards making a perfect ftyle. Milton's profe is in
general very nervous, but it is not free
from ftiffnefs and affectation.

The other period is that of Addifon.
He was undoubtedly one of our fmootheft
and beft writers ; he had the fkill of
uniting eafe, with correctnefs, and more
improved the language than the united
labour

labours of fifty years before him.—
But yet, there were fome little remains of
barbarifm ftill left, which are evident
enough in his contemporaries, and may
be difcovered even in him, by attending
to the ftyle and not to the matter. Will
you believe that fo elegant a writer has
ufed *authenticalnefs* for *authenticity?*—
You may find this horrid word in his
Dialogues on Medals.

Political difputes, though productive
of fo many bad effects, have lately done
the fame fervice as they did formerly—
they have improved our language. Thofe
in the Adminiftration of Sir Robert
Walpole, but more particularly thefe in
our own times, have occafioned fome of
the moft perfect pieces of writing we have
in our tongue. Though, from the nature of the fubject, the pieces themfelves
can fcarcely exift longer than the difpute which gave them being; yet certainly
their effect upon the language will be felt
when

when the quarrel itfelf is no more, and every thing relating to it forgotten.

Though I have affirmed that our language is more perfect now than in any paft period—yet there is ftill much left in it to be corrected.

Nay, there are faults which arife from an affectation of correctnefs. " This day (fays an advertifement) *were* publifhed Meditations of a filent Senator."—If this be right, then " This day *was* publifhed Love's Frailties," muft be wrong—but the reverfe is the truth. " This day *was* publifhed (*a Book* called) Meditations, &c."——" *was* publifhed (*a Comedy* called) Love's Frailties"—and when the work I am now writing is advertifed, it is not *Thirty Letters* which *are* publifhed, but *a Book is* publifhed with that title.

There are fome defects in all languages, which

which have crept in by degrees, and are
fo fanctified by cuftom, that they can never be corrected. In Englifh there is no
difference in writing, tho' there is in pronouncing, the prefent, and preterperfect
tenfes of the verbs *read*, and *cat*, and
fome others. Some unfuccefsful attempts
have been made to diftinguifh them by
writing *redde* and *ate*. There are more
words in Latin of contrary fignifications,
than, I believe, in any other language.
It is a *defect* if the pronunciation of different words be alike, and a great fault if
fuch pronunciation be the confequence of
a refinement. We now pronounce *fore*
and *four*, the fame; which fometimes
makes an odd confufion. " I will come
to you at three, I can't come *before*"—
and " I will come to you at three, I can't
come *by four*"—are pronounced juft the
fame. This we get by affectedly dropping the *u*. In French *au deffous* and *au
deffus* are too much alike for contrary fignifications. Nature dictates a difference

of

of found for different meanings : the ad-
verbs of negation and affent bear no refemblance to each other in any language ;
and almoft all languages agree in fome
fuch-found as *no* for denial.

The London dialect is the caufe of
many improprieties, which, if they were
only ufed in converfation, would not be
worthy of remark ; but as they have begun to make part of our written language,
they deferve fome animadverfion. To
mention a few. The cuftom among the
common people of adding an *s* to many
words, has, I believe, occafioned its being fixed to fome, by writers of rank,
who on account of their refidence in London did not perceive the impropriety.
They fpeak, and write, *chickens—coals
—acquaintances—affiftances*, &c. *Chicken*
is itfelf the plural of *chick*, as *oxen* is of
ox, *kine (cowen)* is of *cow*, and many
others. *Coals* are properly the ftate of all
fewel after it has ceafed to flame, and

3   before

before it becomes aſhes. *Coal* is the mi-
neral ſo called, which (with *acquaintance* and *aſſiſtance*, being aggregate
nouns) admits of no plural termination.
If I were to ſay a bag of *ſhots*, or *ſands*,
the impropriety would be inſtantly perceived; and yet one is as correct as the
other. A late author of great reputation,
who has taken a ſtrict, nay, a verbal re-
view of the Engliſh language, uſes them
as often as they occur.

As the Londoners ſpeak, ſo they alſo
write *learn* for *teach*; this is a very old
miſtake, and occurs frequently in the
pſalms; *do* for *does* (and the contrary),
ſet for *ſit*, *ſee* for *ſaw*, *tin* for *latten*
(which are two different things as well as
words), *ſulky* for *ſullen*, &c. &c. *'Change*
and *'ſample* have been long admitted de-
nizens.—Even in a dictionary you may
find *million* explained to be a fruit well
known—as perhaps in a future edition
we

we shall be told that *fly* signifies a *coach*, and *dilly* a *chaise*.

The London *phraseology* has also been too hard for English. *I got me up—he sets him down—I got no sleep—I slept none* —such a thing is *a* doing—*a* going— *a* coming—*live* lobsters—*live* cattle—I will call *of* you—do not tell *on* it. All these are written without scruple. Our modern comedies, and the London newspapers, abound so much in this language, that they are scarcely intelligible to one who has never been in the capital. Nay in books for the use of schools, the London dialect is so predominant, that many of the sentences are not to be understood by a country boy, and impossible to be rendered into Latin even by those who do understand them. " I will go and fetch a walk in the Green Park"—I will go get me my dinner," and such jargon is perpetually occurring.

English

Englifh has alfo been corrupted by
London *emphafis* and *accent*—I will not
tire you by quoting examples, of which
a long lift might be made, to prove the
great propenfity of the common people
to thofe defects; and it would be a farther
confirmation of what I advanced, that
men of learning really commit improprieties becaufe their ear is familiarized
to them.   The debates in Parliament,
though certainly the beft fpecimens of
eloquence that the world can produce,
have frequently given birth to barbarifms
which are received into our language, and
remain in it.   Should an eminent fpeaker,
in the hurry of declamation, coin a word,
or ufe a bad phrafe, it is taken up by
others upon his authority.   There is
fcarcely a feffion that does not produce
fomething of this fort, which getting into
the public papers, fpreads over the kingdom, and foon becomes fixed too firmly
to be ever removed.

I have

I have yet fomething to add on this fubject—but I muft caution you from imagining that becaufe I find out the faults of others, I pretend to perfection my-felf. Hogarth fays very properly in his Analyfis of Beauty, " do not look for good drawing in thofe examples which I bring of grace and beauty—they are purpofely neglected—attend to the pre-

LETTER

LETTER XII.

I Sometimes provoke you by sporting with matters which you deem sacred. Homer I know is one of your divinities —may I venture to tell you that I never could find that scale of heroes in the Iliad which critics admire as such a beauty?

Hector is supposed in valour superior to all but Achilles—upon what authority? Ajax certainly beat him in the single combat between them; and there are some instances, tho' I cannot recollect the passages, of his inferiority to others of the Greeks; which brings him down so low as to be scarcely worthy of falling by the arm of Achilles.

It

It is furely a blindnefs more than Ho-
merican, not to fee inconfiftencies in the
Iliad, and it is ridiculous to attempt to
make beauties of them. From many
which might eafily be pointed out, take
one or two as they occur to my memory.
After defcribing Mars as the moft terrible
of beings, and to whom whole armies
are as nothing; what *poetical* belief is
ftrong enough to fuppofe he could be
made to retire by Diomed? If Minerva's
fhield is fo vaft (the fhell of a Kraken,
I fuppofe), can one help wondering why
fhe does not ufe it as the King of Laputa
does his ifland, when his fubjects on
Terra-Firma rebel? It is not the hyper-
bole that offends, but the inconfiftency.
The poet had a right to form, and to
endue his gods with what properties he
pleafed—he made them all-powerful; of
courfe, refiftance from mere mortals is
ridiculous and impoffible.

Milton

Milton alfo falfifies his fcale of Hero-
ifm.——Satan, to preferve confiftency,
fhould be fuperior to all excepting
Michael, and yet he is foiled by Abdiel.
If Angels are to be confidered as fpirits,
all fighting is ridiculous and abfurd, becaufe they cannot receive hurt from wea-
pons, and for many other reafons. If
they are to fight upon the principle of
human beings; each muft depend upon
fuperior might and valour, and the moft
powerful ought to overcome. If Abdiel
fubdues Satan by divine affiftance, then
from the fame caufe he might have fingly
encountered and defeated the whole rebel
army. By mixing the fpiritual with the
corporeal nature, the poet has given his
Angels properties which cannot exift together.

But on another occafion, Milton has
with much addrefs prevented an inconfiftency which feemed to be unavoidable.
When

When Gabriel meets Satan in Paradife, every event and reply promifes an imme-diate combat : the " horrid fray" is pre-vented by a circumftance which moft rea-ders would think an ingenious improve-ment on the golden fcales of Homer and Virgil. Voltaire quarrels with the whole incident, and calls the breaking off the fight a difappointment, and the man-ner by which it is done, puerile. But furely it is more confiftent to hinder the encounter, than to bring on a contention which muft either have deftroyed the late creation, or leffened our idea of the might of the combatants.—Nay, I will go far-ther—if it had been confiftent with the character of the Angels to have fought, and this globe to have remained unhurt ; it is better to prevent the combat, as it would have anticipated the war of the Angels in the fixth book, where there is alfo a fingle combat, which has a greater effect by being kept diftinct from other incidents of the fame kind.

So

So that our poet deferves praife rather than
cenfure for the conduct of this incident;
which, in my judgment, poffeffes much
originality and beauty.

LETTER

LETTER XIII.

YOU have not done me juſtice—read the memoirs I ſent you *properly* before they are condemned:—what is any book if it be not read in that manner by which it may beſt be underſtood ?

A novel, whoſe merit lies chiefly in the ſtory, ſhould be quickly paſſed through; for the cloſer you can bring the ſeveral circumſtances together, the better. If its merit conſiſts in character and ſentiment, it ſhould be read much ſlower; for the leaſt obvious parts of a character are frequently the moſt beautiful, and the propriety of a ſentiment may eaſily eſcape in a haſty peruſal. Detached thoughts ought to be dwelt on longer than any other manner of writing; for

different

different fubjects quickly following each other, do rather confound than inftruct; but if we allow ourfelves time to reflect, we may underftand the author, and per-haps improve ourfelves. Each thought fhould be confidered, as a text, upon which we ought to make a commentary.

Bayle's manner of writing by text and note is generally decried, but without reafon. When there is a neceffity of proving the affertion by quotation, which was his cafe, no other way can be taken equally perfpicuous. The authorities muft be produced fomewhere—they cannot be in the text, and if they are put at the end of the book, which is the modern fafhion, how much more troublefome are they for reference, than by being at the bottom of the page? The truth is, this is another inftance of ignorance in the method of reading. Bayle, Harris, and other writers of this clafs, fhould have the text read firft, which is quickly dif-patched;

patched; then, begin again and take in the notes. By thefe means you preferve a connection, and judge of the proofs of what is afferted.

I might in other refpects complain of your treating me rather unfairly; indeed, none judge lefs favourably of an author than his intimate friends—their perfonal knowledge of him as a man, deftroys a many delufions to his advantage as an author.—" Who is a hero to his Valet de Chambre?" faid the great Condé, and he might have added, " or to his friends?" Befides the obvious reafon for this, it is moft likely that an author has, in his common converfation, made his friends acquainted with his fentiments long before they are communicated to the public. The confequence is, that to *them* his work is not new; and it is pof- ble that they may take to themfelves part of his merit; for I have known many inftances, where a perfon has been told fome-

fomething by way of information, which he himfelf told the informer.

Permit me to add, tho' without any application to yourfelf, that an author's intimate acquaintance frequently do him more injury than avowed enemies. They fhew fo many apprehenfions on his account—they fo much dread the cenfure he may incur, and the enemies he may create by his new opinions, &c. All this betrays a want of confidence, and is very naturally fet down to their knowing fomething of the author and his works, the world is not acquainted with.

It is certain, that the lefs perfonal acquaintance we have with an author, the greater is our efteem for his productions; we commend thofe the moft, of whom we know the leaft. Upon the publication of the life of Charles the fifth, the praifes due to its merit were liberally beftowed by fome literati who were in

company together. A Scottifhman prefent, not joining with the reft, upon
being afked the reafon, replied—" I
have feen Dr. Robertfon a hundred times
in Edinburgh."

LETTER

LETTER XIV.

`* * * * * * * * * *`

IT is fo cuſtomary to mention Shakeſpeare and Jonſon together, that many
may think them of equal merit, tho' in
different ways. In my opinion, Jonſon
is one of the dulleſt writers I ever read;
and his plays, with ſome few exceptions, the moſt unentertaining I ever ſaw.
His characters neither feem to be portraits, nor formed upon *general* ideas:
we cannot fancy that there ever were or
can be ſuch people. Shakeſpeare's characters, have that appearance of reality
which always has the effect of actual
life, or at leaſt what paſſes for it on the
ſtage. Jonſon has ſome ſhining paſſages now and then, but not enough to
make

make up for his deficiencies. Shakefpeare, on the contrary, abundantly re-
pays us for being fometimes low and
trifling.

His noble negligences teach
What others toil defpair to reach,
He, perfect dancer, climbs the rope,
And balances your fear and hope:
If after fome diftinguifh'd leap,
He drops his pole, and feems to flip;
Straight gathering all his active ftrength,
He rifes higher half his length!

PRIOR.

One of his commentators much ad-
mires his great art in the conftruction of
his verfes—I dare fay they are very perfect; but when reading this divine poet,
it is as much out of my power to think
upon the art of verfe-making, as it is to
confider the beft way of twifting fiddle-
ftrings at a concert. I am not fufficiently
mafter of myfelf to do any thing that requires deliberation: I am hurried away
like

like a leaf in a whirlwind, and dropped at Thebes or Athens, as the poet pleafes!

Although the pleafure arifing from the reprefentation of Shakefpeare's plays is very great, yet the fpeeches which have any thing violent in the expreffion, are generally fo over-acted as to ceafe to be the " mirror of nature"—but this was always the cafe—" Oh! it offends me to the foul, to fee a robuftious periwig-pated * fellow tear a paffion to tatters :"— tho' this is a " lamentable thing," yet it appears to be without remedy. An actor, in a large theatre, is like a picture hung at a diftance, if the touches are delicate, they efcape the fight: both muft be extravagant to be feen at all, and hence the cuftom of the ancients to make ufe of the Perfona and Bufkin.

* By this epithet, it is plain, that periwigs ex-ifted at leaft half a century before the time ufually affigned for their invention.

Acting

Acting has a very different effect in
the stage-box from what it has in the
back of the gallery. In the one, every
thing appears rough and rude, like a
picture of Spagnolet's near the eye; in
the other it is with difficulty that the
play can be made out. Perhaps, the best
place is the front of the first gallery; as
being sufficiently removed to soften these
hardnesses, yet near enough to see and
hear with advantage.

The writing of a play is as much beyond nature as its performance. The
plot must partake of the marvellous, the
characters must be in situations too violent for common life, and speak a language unheard (but on the stage) in mirth
or distress. There is a degree of impro-
bability in the plot of our best tragedies,
when reduced to the standard of nature.
Otway's Orphan, and Venice Preserved;
Rowe's Tamerlane, Fair Penitent, Jane
Shore, and many others, suppose the ex-
istence

iftence of an impoffibility as the foundation for the ftory. To carry on the
plot, fomething is difclofed, which in
real life would be kept fecret; or fome
information withheld which would always be given, and the diftrefs feems to
be *fought for*, not to *happen*. The obfervation from the gallery at the reprefentation of *the Orphan* was natural—" By
the fpeaking of three words all this
might have been prevented."

The plot of the comedies of Con-
greve, Farquhar, Vanbrugh, &c., alfo
confifts of fituations which cannot be
fuppofed, and events, which in the ufual
courfe of things cannot arife. The characters alfo of both tragedy and comedy,
are as far from refembling real people, as
the bufinefs in which they are employed
is out of the tract of common occur-
rences.

Shakefpeare's plots are moftly taken

H   from

from hiftorical facts, or from novels
where the events are not fo improbable as
thofe fabricated for dramatic ufe, but they
are for that reafon 'more or lefs heightened. · Thofe who think that his perfonages
are natural, are deceived. If they were
fo, they would not be fufficiently marked
for ftage-effect. A ftrong proof of this
is in the portrait of Lear, who is " four-
fcore and upward." Were the character
natural, Lear would be beft acted by an
old man: but every one muft inftantly
perceive, that the ftrength as well as the
abilities of the vigour of life are requifite for its due performance. So that
when we commend plays for being
natural, we mean dramatically fo—but
there is a great difference between heigh-
tening a fituation or character which may
exift, or have its foundation in nature,
and that want of nature and foundation
we perceive in moft of the old writers.

I believe it will be found that all plots

3   and

and characters which intereft us in plays are over-charged, and not real nature, but what the dramatic poets and the audience have agreed to confider as fuch. If we hit this point, our piece is perfect; if we come fhort, or exceed, it is flat or bombaft.

LETTER

LETTER XV.

PRINTING was carried to a great degree of perfection foon after its difcovery. The early Italian books are inferior to no modern ones in the effential principles of the art. Although fome preffes kept their credit, yet, by general inattention, at the beginning of this century, printing was brought down to the loweft pitch of barbarifm. Since that time, in London, Paris, Madrid, Parma, and in other cities, arofe a fpirit of improvement, which, if it be on a good principle, may carry the art to its laft degree of perfection; but, if on a bad one, may do much harm, for fplendor fanctions faults in books as well as men.

To be better underftood, let us endeavour to give a flight inveftigation of the

true

true principles of printing, as far as re-
lates to its ufe and beauty: we fhall then
be enabled to judge, whether the grand
editions of fome books lately publifhed,
have really any juft pretenfions to that
fuperiority they feem to challenge.

Types for printing, fhould be made
upon a fcale of aliquot parts, which will
give a proper proportion of height and
breadth to the letters, and a due proportion to each other. If types are not
formed upon a general principle, although each letter may be in itfelf good,
yet they will appear to be of a different
family.

If the proportion be too broad or too
narrow, it will difpleafe; but, if the beft
proportion be departed from, it is better
to contract than to widen the letter.

Should there be any thing peculiar in
the general form of the type, or, if the

ufual

ufual form of any fingle letter be varied, it is always a change for the worfe.

If the colour of the ink, or of the paper, be unufual; or there be any other circumftance that folicits your attention from the author, to fix it upon the book; it is a fault not to be excufed by any pretence to ornament or elegance.

Admitting the truth of thefe principles, (which I do not wifh to apply to particular books), it will be found, that gray ink, that a blue, yellow, or red caft on the paper, are alterations fo evidently for the worfe, as to be incompatible with elegance.—That the types of our modern fplendid books, and moft of the foreign as well, are not formed upon aliquot parts; fo that the letters difagree with each other, and have befides an affected fharpnefs and precifion, which, nothing but the exacteft proportion can excufe.—That Caflon's type is very perfect,

fect, but that in the Glaſgow letter is united every defirable property, being by far the moſt beautiful of any yet invented. Specimens of all the varieties of theſe two laſt may be feen in Chambers's Dictionary, which will fully juſtify the preference here given them.

An acquaintance of ours has correfponded with a writing-maſter many years, not from any regard to the man, but for the pleaſure he takes in ſeeing fine writing. He preferves his letters carefully, and though he *reads* them to none, (perhaps they are ſtill unread by himſelf) he *ſhews* them to all who can reliſh the excellence of a flouriſh " long drawn out."— Our friend's taſte may be ridiculed by thoſe who " hold it a bafenefs to write fair," but yet it is certain that the true form of letters, in writing, is underſtood no where but in England. I never ſaw a ſpecimen of a correct hand either written or engraved, from any other country, that was

upon

upon a right principle. Perhaps it may be objected, that every nation, prejudiced in favour of its own particular manner, will fay the fame thing. Let us examine this.

Modern writing-hand had its rife from an endeavour to form the true letters as they are printed, with expedition. The firft variation from the original, muft be an oblique inftead of a perpendicular fituation, this naturally arifes from the pofition of the hand—the next, a joining of the letters; thefe two neceffarily produce a third, an alteration of the form. So that writing-hand differs from printing in this, that the former is an arrangement of *connected* characters, the latter of *diftinct* ones. The flit in the pen makes the down-ftrokes full, and the up-ftrokes flight, fo that the body of the letter is ftrong, and the joinings weak, as they fhould be. It is moft natural and eafy alfo to hold the pen always in the fame pofition;

by

by which means the full and hair-ftrokes
are always in their right places. Thefe
feem the neceffary confequence of endeavouring to make the letters expeditioufly
with a pen. The ornamental part comes
next to be confidered. For this, it is requifite that the letters fhould be of the
fame fize and diftance—their leaning
fhould be in the fame direction—the joining be, as much as poffible, uniform—
and, laftly, that the fuperadded ornament
of flourifhing, fhould be continued in the
fame pofition of the pen in which it was
firft begun (generally the reverfe of the
ufual way of holding it), and that the
forms be diftinct, flowing, and grace-
ful.

Thefe appear to me the true principles
of writing. Examine the Italian and
French hands by thefe rules, (fome of
the beft fpecimens are the titles of prints,
&c.) and the hand which they ufe will
be found to be unconnected, full of unmeaning

meaning twifts and curlings generally produced by altering the pofition of the pen, and, upon the whole, awkward, ftiff, and ungraceful.

As they *now* write, we *did*, about feventy or eighty years fince ; fo that our prefent beautiful hand is a new one, and by its being ufed no where but in England, I muft conclude it to be an Englifh invention.

Believe me, in my beft writing, and with my beft wifhes, ever

Yours, &c,

LETTER

LETTER XVI.

I Have often reflected with great grief, that there is fcarce any remarkable natural object in the fublime ftyle, of which we have a drawing to be depended on. The cataract of Niagara.—The peak of Teneriffe, we know nothing of, but that the one is the greateft water-fall, and the other the higheft fingle mountain in the world. It is true, Condamine fays, that the Andes far furpafs the peak of Teneriffe ; more than a third—but, it fhould be confidered, that the valley of Quito is 1600 fathoms above the fea, and that it is from the foot of the mountain that the eye judges of its height. The peak of Teneriffe rifes at once, and has, comparatively, but a fmall bafe—fo that, in

appear-

appearance, it is the higheſt of. mountains.

Teneriffe has been aſcended by many, but deſcribed by none, for I cannot call theſe accounts deſcriptions, which would ſuit any other high mountain as well. Indeed, people generally viſit ſuch objects from other motives than a wiſh to ſatisfy curioſity, or increaſe knowledge. A party aſcended this mountain about a hundred years ago—one of the company giving an account of their journey, ſays—'' being at *la Stancha*, while the reſt were ſpending their time *in cards*. &c. I made it my buſineſs to admire the ſtrangeneſs and vaſtneſs of that great body,*'' &c. The

---

* This may ſerve alſo as an additional proof of the great attraction of cards. (See Letter II.) Teneriffe they could ſee but that once—they might at any future time play at cards—but the love of gaming prevailed over curioſity, though it was to be gratified by one of the moſt ſublime objects in nature.

cataract

cataract of Niagara is moſt excellently *deſcribed* by Mr. Kalm ; but all deſcriptions of viſible objects come ſo ſhort of a repreſentation, and are neceſſarily ſo imperfect, that if ten different painters were to read Mr. Kalm's account of this amazing fall, and to draw it from his deſcription, we ſhould have as many different draughts as painters.

There muſt be ſome amazing ſcenes in Norway by Pontoppidan's deſcriptions, and in the Alps by Schuchtzer's ; theſe writers, and many travellers give views of what they apprehend to be curious ; but draughts made without genius, or by genius without practice, can never give ſuch reſemblance as to convey a proper idea of objects. The view of Lombardy from the Alps—the Bay of Naples—the appearance of Genoa from the ſea, &c. &c. are much talked of, but have never been drawn ; or if drawn, not publiſhed.

From

From this general cenfure I fhould ex‑
cept a View of Vefuvius by a pupil of
Vernet's, and two Views of the Giant's
Caufeway in Ireland, but above all, Gaf‑
par Pouffin's Pictures from Tivoli, and
Views of the Glaciers by Pars, fo ad‑
mirably etched and engraved by Woollet.
All thefe have fomething fo characteriftic,
that we may be fure they give a proper
idea of the fcenes from whence they were
taken.

Of the many thoufands that are con‑
ftantly going to the Eaft-Indies, not one
has publifhed a drawing of the Cape of
Good Hope, nor of Adam's Peak in
Ceylon, nor of fifty other remarkable
objects which are feen in that voyage.—
I mean a *pictorefque* view, not a mere
outline for the ufe of navigators, nor the
unmeaning marks of a pencil directed by
ignorance. I greatly fufpect the fo much
commended draughts in Anfon's voyage
to be nothing but outlines filled up at
random;

random; and more than fufpect, that
many defigns in fome late publications of
this fort, are mere inventions at home:
and this is the more to be lamented, as
every care was taken, in the laft inftance,
that fiction might not be obtruded on us
for reality.

Defcription frequently labours at giving an indiftinct idea of an object which
the mind might conceive at once from a
good reprefentation : and yet defcription
has done wonders, efpecially when affifted
by reflection and fentiment.   I fhall give
an inftance from Rouffeau, expreffing
fome beautiful and even pictorefque circumftances, which it is out of the power
of painting to furnifh.

" Non loin d'une montagne coupée
qu'on appelle le Pas-de-l'Echelle, au-
deffous du grand chemin taillé dans le
roc, à l'endroit appellé Chailles court et
bouillonné dans des gouffres affreux, une
petite

petite riviere *qui paroît avoir mis à les creuſer des milliers de ſiecles.* On a bordé le chemin d'un parapet *pour prévenir les malheurs****** Bien appuyé ſur le parapet, j'avançois le nez, & je reſtois là *des heures entieres, entrevoyant de tems en tems* cette écume & cette eau bleue *dont j'entendois le mugiſſement à travers les cris des corbeaux & des oiſeaux de proie qui voloient de roche en roche & de brouſſaille en brouſſaille, à cent toiſes au-deſſous de moi.* Dans les endroits où la pente étoit aſſez unie, & la brouſſaille aſſez claire pour laiſſer paſſer des cailloux, *j'en allois chercher au loin d'auſſi gros que je les pouvois porter, je les raſſemblois ſur le parapet en pile; puis, les lançant l'un après l'autre, je me délectois à les voir rouler, bondir, & voler en mille éclats avant que d'atteindre le fond du précipice.*"

To ſay that the concluſion is equal to the famous verſe deſcribing the fall of the ſtone of Syſiphus, would be as dangerous

gerous as the having a knock from it—
but, in one we perceive the art of the
poet ; and in the other, the fimple, un-
fought-for expreffion of nature.

I   LETTER

LETTER XVII.

IS there not fomething very fanciful in the analogy which fome people have dif-covered between the arts ? I do not deny the *commune quoddam vinculum*, but would keep the principle within its proper bounds.

Poetry and painting, I believe, are only allied to mufic and to each other; but mufic, befides having the above-named ladies for fifters, has aftronomy and geometry for brothers, and grammar —for a coufin, at leaft.

The intervals of an octave have been made to illuftrate the feven primitive rays of light, and the old planetary fyftem. Seven is one of the myftical numbers—

it

it has hidden meanings and connections which are unknown but to thofe who are deep in the fciences—though we all know that there are feven wife mafters, feven wife miftreffes, feven wonders of the Peak, and feven wonders of the world.

Mufic is alfo fuppofed to have a command over the paffions. This is a doctrine of great antiquity, and has exifted to the prefent times. Timotheus in Dryden's ode, infpires Alexander with pity, love, rage, and every other paffion to which the human heart is fubject.

" What paffion cannot mufic raife or quell ?" fays Pope; and the fame thought has been fo often expreffed, and is now fo generally adopted by all poets and writers on this fubject, that it would be a bold attempt to contradict it, were there not an immediate appeal to our experience and feelings, which muft be held fuperior to authority of ever fo long prefcription.

Thus

Thus fupported then, I afk in my turn
—" What paffion *can* mufic raife or
quell?" Whoever felt himfelf affected,
otherwife than with pleafure, at thofe
ftrains which are fuppofed to infpire
grief—rage—joy—or pity? and this, in
a degree, equal to the goodnefs of the
compofition and performance. The effect of mufic, in this inftance, is juft
the fame as of poetry. We attend—are
pleafed—delighted—tranfported—and
when the heart can bear no more, " glow,
tremble, and weep." All thefe are but
different degrees of pure *pleafure*. When
a poet or mufician has produced this laft
effect, he has attained the utmoft in the
power of poetry or mufic.

Tears being a general expreffion of
grief, pain, and pity; and mufic, when
in its perfection, producing them, has
occafioned the miftake of its raifing the
paffions of grief, &c. But tears, in fact,
are nothing but the mechanical effect of

2   every

every ftrong affection of the heart, and
produced by all the paffions ; even joy and
rage. It is this effect, and the pleafur-
able fenfation together, which Offian (ancient or modern as you pleafe) calls " the
joy of grief."—It is this effect, when
produced by fome grand image, which
Dr. Blair, his critic, ftyles the " fublime
pathetic." And this will explain why
the tyrant fhed tears at a tragedy of Eu-
ripides, who was infenfible to the fuffer-
ings of his fubjects.

I have chofen to illuftrate thefe obfervations from poetry rather than from
mufic, becaufe it is more generally underftood, and more eafily quoted ; but
the principle, though powerful in poetry,
is certainly ftrongeft in mufic. Painting
does not imprefs the eye with any fenfation 'of fufficient force to excite this
effect.——I never faw tears fhed by any
perfon looking at a picture——from
hence

hence it may be juftly inferred that the
fenfations from painting are lefs ftrong
and tumultuous than thofe from poetry
and mufic.

Adieu, &c.

LETTER

LETTER XVIII.

YOUR pictures came fafe—my opinion of them you will in part know from the following obfervations, which, though made on another occafion, are equally applicable to this.

There is in landfcape-painting, and novel-writing, a fault committed by fome of the beft artifts and authors, which is as yet unnamed, becaufe perhaps unnoticed ; permit me to call it a *bad affociation*.

In a landfcape, it is not fufficient that
all

all the objects are such as may well be found together.—In a story, it is not enough that the incidents are such as may well happen—it is neceffary in both, that all the circumftances fhould be of the *fame family.*

Suppofe a landfcape had for its fubject one of Gafpar Pouffin's Views of Ti-
‌ voli—now, though there is nothing more natural than to find mills by running water, yet a mill is not an object that can poffibly agree with the other parts of the picture. It is in a lower clafs.

If in a landfcape of Ruyfdale were introduced the ruins of a temple; tho' a temple may be properly placed in a wood near water, yet it does not fuit the ruftic fimplicity of the pictures of this artift. —It belongs to objects of a fuperior clafs. —Give the mill to Ruyfdale and the temple to Gafpar—all will be right.

Thefe

Thefe two painters were the moſt perfect in their different ſtyles that ever exiſted. Both formed themſelves upon the
ſtudy of nature, both were correct, both
excellent; and yet ſo totally different from
each other, that there are ſcarce any parts
of the pictures of the one, that will
bear being introduced into thoſe of the
other.

Claude's magnificent ideas frequently
betrayed him into *a bad affociation.*—
Large grand maſſes of trees agree but ill
with ſea and ſhips, unleſs they are removed to a diſtance. They are objects
of different claſſes.

Lambert, who formed himſelf upon
the ſtudy of Gaſpar, took his trees, rocks,
and other circumſtances from that maſter;
but his buildings from the Gardener's
huts at Newington, which is confounding

ing real grandeur with affected fimplicity*.

A ftory which proceeds upon a regular circumfcribed plan, chiefly confifting
of dialogue and fentiment, where the
fcene is laid in London, and the characters fuch as are natural to the place; has
a bad affociation if the author goes to
Africa in queft of adventures. On the
other hand, a novel which fets out upon
the principle of variety, and where a frequent change of place is neceffary to the
execution of the defign : has *a bad affo-*
ciation if the author in any part of it
quits adventure for fentiment or fatire.
And yet, this has been done by Fielding

* An agreeable and truly diftinguifhing writer
feems fully fenfible of the principle of proper affociation—" A foreft fcene introduced as a picture is
introduced with diftinction, and calls for every ap-
pendage of grandeur, to harmonize with it. The
cottage offends—it fhould be a caftle, a bridge, an
aqueduct, or fome other object that fuits its dignity."

and

and Smollet, two of our beſt novel-
writers, who, either from not knowing
this principle, or not attending to it,
have mixed circumſtances which ſhould
have been kept diſtinct, as they belong
to claſſes of writing which cannot accord
together.

LETTER

LETTER XIX.

THERE never was a poet more admired in his life, or more defpifed after his death than Quarles. He was patronized by the beft of his age while living; and when dead, was firft criticized, then con-temned, and at laft totally forgotten, un-lefs fome bard wanted a name of one fyllable to fill up a lift of miferable rhymers. Pope was the laft who made. this ufe of him, and at the fame time in a note cenfured Benlowes for being his patron.

I think it is Sir Philip Sidney who fays, that no piece was ever a favourite of the common people without merit.

Now,

Now, though every thing I had heard of Quarles was much in his disfavour, I conceived that he might have fomething good in him, from my never feeing one of his books of Emblems that was not worn to rags; a fign of its being read a good deal, unlefs it may be imagined that it was fo ufed by children in turning over the prints.

Be that as it may, I have perufed as much of him as a very dirty tattered book would permit, and will rifque the declaring, that where he is good, I know but few poets better. He has much genuine fire, is frequently happy in fimiles, admirable in epithets and compound words; fmooth in his verfification, fo unlike the poets of his own age; and poffeffed that great qualification of keeping you in perpetual alarm, fo very different from the elegant writers of the prefent times.

I have

I have run through his book of Emblems to felect fome paffages for your
obfervation—they are buried, it muft be
confeffed, in a heap of rubbifh, but are
of too much value not to be worth fome
pains in recovering.—Where Quarles is
bad, " he founds the very bafe-ftring of
humility"—but this may with equal
truth be faid of Shakefpeare and Milton.
I mean not to put him in the fame rank
with thefe two great poets; he has a
much greater proportion of bad than is
to be found in them, fo much indeed, as
almoft to prevent the good from appearing at all*. My intention is to clear
fome of his fhining paffages of their in-
cumbrances; which may occafion their
being noticed, and preferved from oblivion.

* Notwithftanding this plain affertion, the author
has been confidered as an indifcriminate admirer of
Quarles—from the fame principle he may be confidered as a cenfurer of Milton and Shakefpeare—the
one is as true as the other.

What

What think you of the following fimilies?

Look how the ftricken hart that wounded flies
O'er hills and dales, and feeks the lower grounds
For running ftreams, the whilft his weeping eyes
    Beg filent mercy * from the following hounds;
At length, emboft, he droops, drops down, and lies
    Beneath the burthen of his bleeding wounds:
Ev'n fo my gafping foul, diffolv'd in tears, &c.
Emb. 11. Book IV.

Mark how the widow'd turtle, having loft
    The faithful partner of her loyal heart,
Stretches her feeble wings from coaft to coaft,
    Hunts ev'ry path; thinks ev'ry fhade doth part
Her abfent love and her; at length, unfped,
    She re-betakes her to her lonely bed,
And there bewails her everlafting widow-hed †.
Emb. 12. Book IV.

Look

* Although this circumftance has been often remarked, there feems a particular refemblance between this paffage and one in Cotton's tranflation of
Montaigne.—" It frequently happens that the ftag
we hunt, finding himfelf weak and out of breath,
feeing no other remedy, furrenders himfelf to us
who purfue him, *imploring mercy by his tears.*"

————queftuque cruentus
    Atque imploranti fimilis.

† John Harington in a letter to his fifter, written
in

Look how the sheep, whose rambling steps do stray
From the safe blessing of her shepherd's eyes,
Eftsoon becomes the unprotected prey
  To the wing'd squadron of beleag'ring flies;
Where sweltered with the scorching beams of day
  She frisks from bush to brake, and wildly flies away
From her own self, ev'n of herself afraid;
  She shrouds her troubled brows in ev'ry glade,
And craves the mercy of the soft removing shade.

EMB. 14. BOOK IV.

The first will probably remind you of Shakefpeare's description of the wounded stag in *As you like it*; which it may do, and not suffer by the comparison. The second, is very original in the expression —the circumstance of

in 1647, puts this and the following stanza into prose:

" Doth not the widow'd turtle, lost to the faithful partner of her heart, stretch forth her feeble wing from coast to coast, in haunt of every path! at last betakes her to the lonely bed."

" Mark how the simple sheep, whose rambling steps do stray from the safe blessing of her shepherd's eye, becomes the unprotected prey of night-howling wolves; she frisks from bush to brake, &c."

———thinks

————— thinks every *ſhade* doth part
Her abſent love and her ————

is I believe new, and exquiſitely tender.
There are others not much inferior to
theſe,

The following verſes allude to the
print prefixed, where a bubble is repreſented as heavier than the globe, It is
neceſſary to obſerve, that the prints were
deſigned firſt, and the poems were in a
great meaſure explanatory of them.

Lord! what a world is this, which day and night
  Men ſeek with ſo much toil, with ſo much trouble,
Which weigh'd in equal ſcales is found ſo light,
  So poorly overbalanc'd, with a bubble ?
    Good God! that frantic mortals ſhould deſtroy
    Their higher hopes, and place their idle joy
Upon ſuch airy traſh, upon ſo light a toy!
  * * * *

Thrice happy he, whoſe nobler thoughts deſpiſe
  To make an objeƈt of ſo eaſy gains;
Thrice happy he, who ſcorns ſo poor a prize
  Should be the crown of his heroic pains:

K   Thrice

Thrice happy he, that ne'er was born to try
Her frowns or smiles: or being born, did lie
In his sad nurse's arms an hour or two, and die.

Emb. 4. Book I.

Although mortality confidered on the gloomy fide, is not productive of much happinefs, yet there are certain difpofitions which feel fome gratification in it —Quarles was one of thefe. He feizes all opportunities of abufing the world; and it muft be confefled he has here done it in " choice and elegant terms."

Sometimes he is more outrageous in his abufe.

Let wit, and all her ftudied plots effect
    The beft they can;
Let fmiling fortune profper and perfect
    What wit began;
Let earth advife with both, and fo project
    A happy man;
Let wit or fawning fortune vie their beft;
    He may be bleft
With all that earth can give; but earth
    Can give no reft.

Emb. 6. Book I.

3   Again

‛Again——

> Falſe world, thou ly'ſt : thou can'ſt not lend
> The leaſt delight :
> Thy favours cannot gain a friend,
> They are ſo ſlight :
> Thy morning-pleaſures make an end
> To pleaſe at night : ˌ
> Poor are the wants that thou ſupply'ſt :
> And yet thou vaunt'ſt, and yet thou vy'ſt
> With heav'n —— —— ——.
>
> EMB. 5. BOOK II.

The next quotation is an alluſion to the print, where the world is made a mirror.

> Believe her not, her glaſs diffuſes
> Falſe portraitures ————
> Were thy dimenſions but a ſtride,
> Nay, wert thou ſtatur'd but a ſpan,
> Such as the long-bill'd troops defy'd,
> A very fragment of a man!
>
> Had ſurfeits, or th' ungracious ſtar
> Conſpir'd to make one common place
> Of all deformities that are
> Within the volume of thy face,
> She'd lend the favour ſhou'd out-move
> The Troy-bane Helen, or the Queen of Love.
>
> EMB. 6. BOOK II.

This

This is finely wrought up—Quarles perfectly comprehended the effect of the mufical *crefcendo*, which is inftanced particularly in the laft paffage.

There is fomething very dreadful in the 4th line of this ftanza.

> See how the latter trumpet's dreadful blaft
> Affrights ftout Mars his trembling fon!
> See how he ftartles! how he ftands aghaft,
> And fcrambles from his melting throne!
> Hark! how the direful hand of vengeance tears
> The fwelt'ring clouds, whilft Heav'n appears
> A circle fill'd with flame, and center'd with his fears
> EMB. 9. BOOK II.

Dr. Young has fome lines on this fubject which are much admired.—But though the fubject be the fame, it is differently circumftanced.—Young's is a general defcription of the laft judgment, Quarles defcribes its effect on a fingle being who is fuppofed to have lived fearlefs of fuch an event.

——————At

———————— At the deftin'd hour,
By the loud trumpet fummon'd to the charge,
See all the formidable fons of fire,
Eruptions, earthquakes, comets, lightnings, play
Their various engines; all at once difgorge
Their blazing magazines; and take by ftorm
This poor terreftrial citadel of man.
Amazing period! when each mountain height
Out-burns Vefuvius! rocks eternal pour
Their melted mafs, as rivers once they pour'd;
Stars rufh, and final *Ruin* fiercely drives
Her plough-fhare o'er creation.————

Now to me, all this is a " peftilent con-
gregation of vapour."—The formidable
fons of fire fpewing out blazing magazines—and *Ruin*, like a plough-man
(or rather plough-woman) driving *her*
plough-fhare—are mean, incoherent images. How much more fublimely Quarles
expreffes the fame, and indeed fome additional ones, in the laft three lines?

In the print belonging to the emblem
from which the following paffage is
taken,

taken, is a figure ftriking a globe with
his knuckles.—The motto, *Tinnit, inane
eft.*

She's empty—hark! fhe founds—there's nothing there
    But noife to fill thy ear;
Thy vain enquiry can at length but find
    A blaft of murm'ring wind:
It is a cafk, that feems as full as fair
    But merely tunn'd with air;
Fond youth, go build thy hopes on better grounds:
    The foul that vainly founds
Her joys upon this world, but feeds on empty founds!
              EMB. 10. BOOK II.

That you may not think the good
paffages of this poet are but fcattered un-
equally through his poems; take fome
entire ones—or nearly fo.

What fullen ftar rul'd my untimely birth,
That would not lend my days one hour of mirth?
How oft' have thefe bare knees been bent to gain
The flender alms of one poor fmile in vain?
How often, tir'd with the faftidious light,
Have my faint lips implor'd the fhades of night?
How often have my nightly torments pray'd
For ling'ring twilight, glutted with the fhade?
                        Day

Day worfe than night, night worfe than day appears,
In fighs I fpend my nights, my days in tears:
I moan unpity'd, groan without relief:
There is no end nor meafure of my grief.
The fmiling flow'r falutes the day; it grows
Untouch'd with care; it neither fpins nor fows:
O that my tedious life were like this flow'r,
Or freed from grief, or finifh'd with an hour:
Why was I born? why was I born a man?
And why proportioned by fo large a fpan?
Or why fufpended by the common lot,
And being born to die, why die I not?
Ah me! why is my forrow-wafted breath
Deny'd the eafy privilege of death?
The branded flave that tugs the weary oar,
Obtains the fabbath of a welcome fhore.
His ranfom'd ftripes are heal'd: his native foil
Sweetens the mem'ry of his foreign toil:
But ah! my forrows are not half fo bleft;
My labour finds no point, my pains no reft.
* * * * * *

Thou juft obferver of our flying hours,
That with thy adamantine fangs, devours
The brazen mon'ments of renowned kings,
Doth thy glafs ftand? or be thy moulting wings
Unapt to flie? if not, why doft thou fpare
A willing breaft; a breaft that ftands fo fair?
A dying breaft, that hath but only breath
To beg the wound, and ftrength to crave a death?
O that the pleafed heav'ns would once diffolve
Thefe flefhly fetters, that fo faft involve

My

My hamper'd foul; then would my foul be blest
From all thofe ills, and wrap her thoughts in reft!

* * * * * *

Emb. 15. Book III.

At other times he complains of the
fhortnefs of life, and in ftrains equally
pathetic.

My glafs is half unfpent; forbear t' arreft
My thriftlefs day too foon : my poor requeft
Is that my glafs may run but out the reft.

My time-devoured minutes will be done
Without thy help; fee—fee how fwift they run:
Cut not my thread before my thread be fpun.

The gain's not great I purchafe by this ftay ;
What lofs fuftain'ft thou by fo fmall delay,
To whom ten thoufand years are but a day ?

My following eye can hardly make a fhift
To count my winged hours; they fly fo fwift,
They fcarce deferve the bounteous name of gift.

The fecret wheels of hurrying time do give
So fhort a warning, and fo faft they drive,
That I am dead before I feem to live.

And what's a life ? a weary pilgrimage,
Whofe glory in one day doth fill the ftage
With childhood, manhood, and decrepit age.

And

1

And what's a life! the flourishing array
Of the proud summer-meadow, which to-day
Wears her green plush, and is to-morrow hay.

Read on this dial, how the shades devour
My short-liv'd winter's day; hour eats up hour;
Alas! the total's but from eight to four.

Behold these lilies, which thy hands have made
Fair copies of my life, and open laid
To view, how soon they droop, how soon they fade!

Shade not that dial, night will blind too soon;
My non-aged day already points to noon;
How simple is my suit! how small my boon!

Nor do I beg this slender inch, to while
The time away, or falsely to beguile
My thoughts with joy; here's nothing worth a smile.

No, no, 'tis not to please my wanton ears
With frantic mirth; I beg but hours, not years:
And what thou giv'st me, I will give to tears!
* * * * * *

EMB. 13. BOOK III.

" Read on *this* dial"—" Behold *these*
lilies"—does not this put you in mind of
the same form of expression in Offian?
" His spear was like *that* blasted fir."

Quarles

Quarles was commenting on his print in which the dial and lilies were repre-fented; Offian faw his images "in his mind's eye"—but both the poets con-fidered them as really exifting—at leaft, they make them exift to their readers. Perhaps you fmile at my quoting Offian as a real poet—the expreffion is poetical, whoever be the author.

"How the fhades devour," &c. Shakefpeare has the fame figure :

———————— the tide
Eats not the flats with more impetuous hafte——

it is wonderfully expreffive !

In what he calls his hieroglyphics, Quarles compares man to a taper, which furnifhes him with a number of very ftriking allufions. It is at firft unlighted, then a hand from heaven touches it with fire—the motto, *Nefcius unde.*

This

This flame-expecting taper hath at length
  Received fire, and now begins to burn :
It hath no vigour yet, it hath no ftrength ;
    Apt to be puft and quencht at every turn :
      It was a gracious hand that thus endow'd
      This fnuff with flame : but mark, this hand doth
        fhroud
Itfelf from mortal eyes, and folds it in a cloud.

Thus man begins to live. An unknown-flame
  Quickens his finifhed organs, now poffeft
With motion ; and which motion doth proclaim
    An active foul, though in a feeble breaft : .,
      But how, and when infus'd, afk not my pen ;
      Here flies a cloud before the eyes of men,
I cannot tell thee how, nor canft thou tell me when.

Was it a parcel of celeftial fire,
  Infus'd by heav'n into this flefhly mould ?
Or was it, think you, made a foul entire ? .
    Then, was it new created, or of old ?
      Or is't a propagated fpark, rak'd out
      From nature's embers ; while we go about
By reafon to refolve, the more we raife a doubt.

If it be part of that celeftial flame,
  It muft be ev'n as pure, as free from fpot,
As that eternal fountain whence it came ;
    If pure and fpotlefs, then whence came the blot ?
      Itfelf being pure, could not itfelf defile ;
      Nor hath unactive matter pow'r to foil]
Her pure and active form, as jars corrupt their oil.

Or

Or if it were created, tell me when?
If in the firſt ſix days, where kept till now?
Or if thy ſoul were new-created, then
　Heav'n did not all at firſt, he had to do;
　Six days expired, all creation ceaſt;
　All kinds, ev'n from the greateſt to the leaſt,
Were finiſh'd and compleat before the day of reſt.

But why ſhould man, the Lord of creatures, want
　That privilege which plants and beaſts obtain?
Beaſts bring forth beaſts, and plant a perfect plant;
And ev'ry like brings forth her like again:
　Shall fowls and fiſhes, beaſts and plants convey
　Life to their iſſue, and man leſs than they?
Shall theſe get living ſouls, and man dead lumps of clay?

Muſt human ſouls be generated then?—
　My water ebbs; behold a rock is nigh:
If nature's work produce the ſouls of men,
　Man's ſoul is mortal—all that's born muſt die.
　What ſhall we then conclude! what ſunſhine will
　Diſperſe this gloomy cloud? till then, be ſtill
My vainly ſtriving thoughts; lie down my puzzled quill.
HIEROGLYPH. 2.

The cloſeneſs of the reaſoning, and
the freedom of the verſes cannot be
enough admired. I believe it would be
difficult, if not impoſſible, to reaſon ſo
ſhortly, and yet ſo clearly in proſe. Pope
ſays,

[141]

ſays, the thoughts in his Eſſay on Man
are more compreſſed by being in verſe—
Poetical language admitting of eliſions,
and other varieties, inconſiſtent with the
character of proſe.

This poem is followed by another,
before which is a deſign of the winds
blowing the flame of the taper, with this
motto, " *The wind paſſeth over it, and
it is gone!*"

    No ſooner is this lighted Taper ſet
      Upon the tranſitory ſtage
        Of eye-bedark'ning night,
    But it is ſtraight ſubjected to the threat
      Of envious winds, whoſe waſteful rage
        Diſturbs her peaceful light,
And makes her ſubſtance waſte, and makes her flame
            [leſs bright.

    No ſooner are we born, no ſooner come
      To take poſſeſſion of this vaſt,
        This ſoul-afflicting earth,
    But danger meets us at the very womb;
      And ſorrow with her full-mouth'd blaſt
        Salutes our painful birth
To put out all our joys, and puff out all our mirth.

                  Nor

Nor infant innocence, nor childifh tears,
  Nor youthful wit, nor manly pow'r,
    Nor politic old age,
Nor virgins pleading, nor the widow's pray'rs,
  Nor lowly cell, nor lofty tow'r,
    Nor prince, nor peer, nor page,
Can 'fcape this common blaft, nor curb her ftormy rage.
* * * * * *

Toft to and fro, our frighted thoughts are driv'n
  With ev'ry puff, with ev'ry tide
    Of life-confuming care;
Our peaceful flame, that would point up to heav'n
  Is ftill difturb'd and turn'd afide;
    And ev'ry blaft of air
Commits fuch wafte in man, as man cannot repair.
* * * * * *

What may this forrow-fhaken life prefent
  To the falfe relifh of our tafte
    That's worth the name of fweet?
Her minute's pleafure's choak'd with difcontent,
  Her glory foil'd with ev'ry blaft—
    How many dangers meet
Poor man betwixt the biggin and the winding fheet!
                                HIEROGLYPH. 3.

Tho' I have purpofely omitted point-
ing out many of the particular beauties
of thefe poems, I would wifh you to
                                          obferve,

obferve, in this laft, the fine effect of
compound words in which this author is
fo happy: alfo the noble fwell in the
third ftanza—the application of his al-
legory to its meaning, in the fourth,
where the expreffion fo admirably ac-
cords with both, " *our peaceful flame* *,"
&c.—if thefe are not genuine ftrokes of
genius, I muft, as a great critic fays on
a like occafion, acknowledge my ignorance of fuch fubjects. I wifh we had
fome word in our language to exprefs
the fame idea in poetry as *crefcendo* does
in mufic; *fwell* is applied to fo many
other purpofes, that it has not the effect
of an appropriated term.

* An author, who probably knew nothing of
Quarles, has made a beautiful ufe of this figure—

" Une religion pure, aidée par des mœurs chaftes,
les dirigeoit vers une autre vie comme la flamme qui
s'envole vers le ciel lorfqu'elle n'a plus d'aliment fur
la terre."

But

But for the prefent I muft quit the
fubject—in a little time expect the remainder of my obfervations on this
poet.

LETTER

LETTER XX.

EVERY one feems to be fatisfied that warm colouring is effential to a good picture: but what *is* warm colouring is not determined. Some have joined the idea of warmth to yellow, others to red, others to the compound of both, the orange—they alfo differ in the degrees of each. A warm picture to fome, is cold to others; and vice verfa. Lambert's idea of warmth, was to make his pictures appear as if they were behind a yellow glafs. Vanbloom's have a red glafs before them. Both's an orange colour. Each has its admirers, who condemn the reft.

Who fhall decide when Doctors difagree?

L   Nature.

Nature. All thefe hues are right as *particulars*, but wrong as *univerfals*.

Let us examine the different appear-ances of light from the dawn to noon. The firft break of day is a cold light in the Eaft—this, by degrees, is tinged with purple, which grows redder and redder until the purple is loft in orange— the orange in yellow, and before the fun is two degrees high, the yellow is chang-ed to white. Invert the order of thefe, and it is the coming on of the evening. All thefe hues then exift in nature, and one is as proper as the other.

It is neceffary to diftinguifh between the painter's *warmth*, and the fenfation. A picture, poffeffing moft warmth of colouring, reprefents that time of the day when we feel leaft. A true repre-fentation of noon muft have no tinge of yellow or red in the fky; and yet from its being noon, one might be led to ima-gine

gine it muſt be *warm*. It is the critic,
and not the artiſt, who confounds the
meaning of theſe terms.

In like manner, ſummer and winter,
in reſpect to light, are the ſame; the
ſun riſes and ſets as gorgeouſly in De-
cember, if the weather be clear, as in
June. I remember ſeeing two pictures
of Cuyp, companions—one, a cattle
piece in ſummer; the other, winter with
figures ſkaiting. The ſky in both was
equally *warm*, for which the painter was
much cenſured by an auction-connoiſſeur,
who declared that it was impoſſible the
ſky could be *warm* in winter.

I believe it is a common miſtake, to
apply the red and purple tints to the
morning, and the orange and yellow to
the evening. We hear pictures of Claude
called mornings and evenings, which
may be either. It is really odd enough,
that there ſhould not be a ſingle circum-

ſtance

stance to distinguish the morning from
the evening, unless it be in a view of a
particular place—in this cafe, the reverfing of the light shews the difference.
In a picture, there is no distinction between going to, and returning from
work, or milking—men ride, drive cattle, are fishing, &c. as well early as
late *.

Thefe

* An accurate judge of thefe fubjects remarks,
that " Landfcape painters, in general, pay too little
attention to the difcriminations of morning and
evening.—We are often at a lofs to diftinguifh in
pictures the rifing from the fetting fun, tho' their
characters are very different both in the lights and
fhadows. The ruddy lights indeed of the evening
are more eafily diftinguifhed: but it is not perhaps
always fufficiently obferved, that the fhadows of the
evening are much lefs opaque than thofe of the
morning. They may be brightened, perhaps, by
the numberlefs rays floating in the atmofphere,
which are inceffantly reverberated in every direction; and may continue in action after the fun is
fet. Whereas in the morning, the rays of the preceding day having fubfided, no object receives any
light,

'Thefe confiderations fhould foften the peremptory ftyle of critics by profeffion, and extend their tafte, which at prefent feems much confined. A picture may be too warm, too cold, too red, too yellow, to pleafe an eye partial to a particular tint—but it ought to be remembered that all thefe hues are natural, and, in the hands of a real artift, all pictorefque.

light, but from the immediate luftre of the fun. Whatever becomes of the theory, the fact, I believe, is well afcertained."   GILPIN.

To endeavour the eftablifhing my own opinion by confuting the doctrine advanced in this quotation, would be to depart from the principle I fixed for my conduct in the Advertifement prefixed to thefe Letters. But, doubtlefs, upon a revifal of this paffage, the ingenious author will perceive that a different opacity of fhadows for morning and evening, as far as the art of painting is concerned, is merely ideal—and not lefs fo than the unphilofophical notion with which it is fupported.

LETTER

LETTER XXI.

AT the revival of the arts, fome evil genius, determined to retard the progrefs of painting, dictated this rule. " A picture fhould always have its horizon the height of the eye *that looks at it—* in nature, the eye being always the height of the horizon; therefore a picture will be moft like nature that has its horizon the height of the *natural eye.*" One of the falfeft rules that ever was founded on a falfe principle ! and the more lamentable, as it has fpoiled, in point of perfpective, three parts of the hiftorical pictures that have ever been painted.

As it is very difficult to deftroy a rooted error, and as this is a moft per-
nicious

nicious one, it is neceffary to be full and particular.

When I fay *eye* and *horizon*—the natural eye and horizon are meant. When the terms *artificial eye* and *artificial horizon* are ufed, the eye and the horizon reprefented in painting are to be under-ftood. We muft be clear in this diftinction, for it is the confounding of the ideas expreffed by thefe terms which has occafioned the mifchief.

The eye, and the horizon, are always of the fame height—therefore

The artificial eye and the artificial horizon muft always be fo—but

There is no connection between the *real* eye, and the *artificial* horizon.

In every picture the artificial eye, or point

point of fight, is fuppofed to be at a
certain height from the bafe-line; as
high as a human figure would be, repre-
fented as ftanding there. To this point
every thing in the picture tends, as every
thing in a real view tends to the natural
eye. The picture then, as far as this
circumftance is concerned, is perfect, if
the *artificial* eye and the *artificial* horizon
go together; for thefe always bear the
fame relation to each other, let the picture be placed any where.

Let

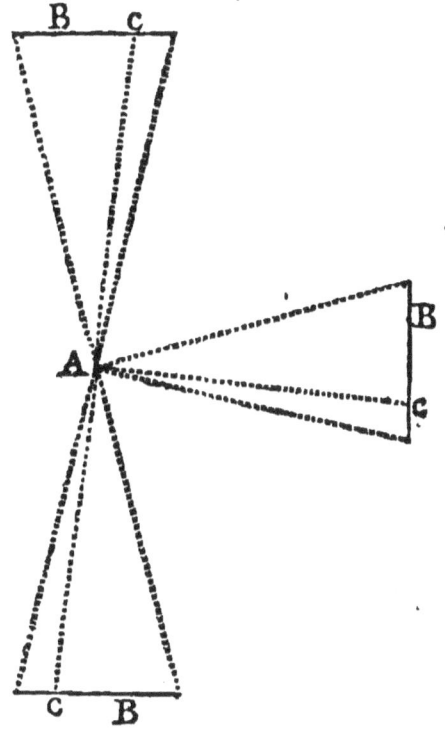

Let A be the eye, B the picture (in
section) and c the horizon of the picture.
—The eye is always the apex of the
cone; there is constantly the same relation between the parts, in every position.
It must be observed, that there is a defect

3

fect in this illuftration which it was impoffible to avoid—for tho' I have confidered A as the eye, yet *upon paper*, it
is *artificial* as well as the picture B. If
you cannot make this diftinction, I pro-
pofe the following demonftration.——
Take a landfcape and ftand it upon a ta-
ble—hang it up the height of the eye—
above the height—put it upon a chair—
upon the floor—it ftill, perfpectively
confidered, is feen equally well—for

The *real* eye is always the height of
the *artificial* eye, whether the picture be
fixed in the cieling or laid upon the floor.
Indeed if this was not fo, how would
it be poffible to hang one picture over
another ? and yet this is done, and with
the greateft propriety.

I have often lamented the fhifts to
which painters are reduced, who have
followed this rule in oppofition to their
fenfes.

fenfes. Lareffe was fo thoroughly poffeffed with it, that his idea of fitting up
a room with pictures, was to have thofe
which were below the eye to contain nothing but ground, and thofe which were
above, the fky and clouds. But though
he was convinced of the rectitude of his
principle, he was ftruck with the oddity
of the practice—he therefore · recom-
mended that there fhould be but one
picture from the floor to the cieling, in
which there might be a perfect coincidence of the natural and artificial horizon.

A portrait-painter fets the perfon he is
to draw, generally the height of his eye.
—Suppofe it to be a whole-length with
a landfcape in the back-ground: the
artift confiders his picture is to hang
above the eye, and for that reafon makes
his horizon low, about the height of the
knees. The confequence is, that there
are two points of fight, which fuppofes

an

an impoffibility; for the eye cannot be in two places at the fame time. If the eye be fuppofed on a level with the head of the figure, as it was on drawing the face, then the back-ground is too low; if equal to the horizon of the back-ground, then the figure is too high, un-lefs we fuppofe it on an eminence, or ourfelves in a pit; in that cafe, inftead of feeing the face in front, we muft have looked under the chin—but as we do not, the figure always appears to be falling forward.

Raffaele's horizon is commonly the height of his figures, fo that they ftand properly, and feem to be, whether in a print or a picture, the fize of human creatures;—on the contrary, when the horizon is low, the figures always appear gigantic. In early life, I had formed fo very exalted an idea of the fize of run-ning horfes, from feeing them drawn with the diftant hills appearing under

their

their bodies, that the firſt time I was at
a courſe, it appeared a mere rat-race.

Every whole-length piƈture will fur-
niſh you with an inſtance of this falſe
principle, which would appear more diſ-
agreeable, if we were not in ſome meaſure reconciled to it by cuſtom. I am
aware that the praƈtice of ſo many great
men is a ſtrong objeƈtion to my argu-
ment ; but as the principle is ill founded,
there ought to be no objeƈtion to its
being abandoned.

LETTER

LETTER XXII.

THE commentators of Shakefpeare think themfelves obliged to find fome meaning in his nonfenfe; and to come at it, twift and turn his words without mercy: never confidering, that in his fcenes, as in common life, fome part muft be neceffarily unimportant.

Many a paffage has been criticifed into confequence. The meaning, to ufe the Poet's words on a like occafion, " is like a grain of wheat hid in a bufhel of chaff; you fhall feek all day ere you find it, and when you have it, it is not worth the fearch."

An expreffion of Juftice *Shallow's* in the fecond part of Henry the Fourth has been

been the fubject of much criticifm and
hypercriticifm. "We will eat a laft
year's pippin with a difh of carraways;"
and it is certain that there was fuch a
difh; but if Shakefpeare had meant it,
he would have faid, "A difh of laft
year's pippins with carraways"—" *with*
a difh, &c." clearly means fomething
diftinct from the pippins. Roafted pippins ftuck full of carraways, fays one—
carraway confect, or comfit well known
to children, fays another—as if every
one did not know what carraway com-
fits were, fays a third, laughing at the
fecond. Dine with any of the *natural*
inhabitants of Bath about Chriftmas, and
they probably will give you after dinner
a difh of pippins and carraways—which
laft, is the name of an apple as well
known in that country, as nonpareil is
in London, and as generally affociated
with golden pippins.

"Then am I a fous'd gurnet," fays
Falftaff.

Falftaff. This fifh has puzzled the
commentators as much as the apple did
before.—What can it be?—I never heard
of fuch a fifh.—There is no fuch fifh.
A magazine critic, affured of its non-
exiftence, propofed reading *grunt*; gurnet, quafi grunet, quafi grunt—well, and
what do we get by that? Why, becaufe
hogs grunt, and pork is the flefh of
hogs, fous'd gurnet means pickled pork!
Very lately, a commentator, who once
denied its exiftence, has difcovered, in
confequence of his great learning, that
there is *really* fuch a fifh——he is *really*
in the right—if he will go to the South
coaft of Devonfhire, he may fee plenty
of them—but not *fous'd.*

And now I mention Falftaff, let me
explain his copper ring. He complains
of being robbed when he was afleep,
and "lofing a feal-ring of his *grandfather's* worth forty marks." "O Jefu,"
fays the hoftefs, "I have heard the
prince

prince tell him I know not how oft, that the ring was *copper*." Is the appearance of copper fo much like gold, that one may be miftaken for the other? Formerly, (about the time of Falftaff's grandfather) gold was a fcarce commodity in England, fo fcarce, that they frequently made rings of copper, and plated them thinly with gold; I have feen two or three of them. As the look of both was alike, Falftaff might infift upon its being gold; on the contrary, the prince, from the quality of the wearer and lightnefs of the ring, might with equal fairnefs maintain that it was only plated.

Though it is not my intention to make one of the number of Shakefpeare's commentators, I will take this opportunity of reftoring a paffage in King Lear. In the agony of his paffion with his daughter, he fays (in the modern editions)

" Th'

" Th' *untented* woundings of a Father's curfe
Pierce every fenfe about thee."

In the old editions it is printed exceeding
plainly, " Th' *untender* woundings," &c.
that is, *not tender*, or *cruel*. It would
be wafte of time to fhew its propriety,
and that there is no fuch word as *untented*. Who firft threw out the true
reading and fubftituted the falfe, I know
not. The word is often ufed by Shakefpeare, and once at leaft befides in the
fame play, " fo young and fo *untender ?*"

One more and I will releafe you.—
Shylock fays,

Some men there are, love not a gaping pig;
Some that are mad, if they behold a cat;
And others, when the bag-pipe fings in the nofe,
Cannot contain, &c.——for *affection*.

that is, becaufe they are fo *affected*.
Thefe poor lines have been new worded,
new ftopped, and all to. find the meaning

ing of as plain a paſſage as can be written. " Some men cannot abide this
thing, others have an averſion to another, which ſometimes produces ſtrange
effeᶜts on their bodies, becauſe their
imagination is ſo ſtrongly *affeᶜted*. Maſ-
terlefs paſſion (that is, a ſuffering or
feeling which cannot be overcome) com-
pels them to follow the impulſe." The
not underſtanding *affeᶜtion* and *paſſion* in
Shakeſpeare's quaint ſenſe, has occaſioned the difficulty.

Two qualifications are abſolutely neceſſary for the commentators on our old
poets—being verſed in the authors of the
times—and in the provincial dialeᶜts.
There are many words and phraſes occurring in theſe writers ſtill uſed by the.
common people in the ſame ſenſe as formerly, which would inſtantly explain
paſſages that claſſic learning and modern
refinement labour at in vain.

Two

'Two other qualifications are neceſſary for an editor of Shakeſpeare—a poetical imagination—and a diſcernment to diſtinguiſh what is probable from what is merely poſſible.

If the validity of theſe rules were admitted, and the different critics and commentators tried by them—'' they muſt be uſed better than their deſert to eſcape whipping.''

Shakeſpeare appears more like himſelf in the twenty plays publiſhed from the earlieſt editions (notwithſtanding the many errors of the firſt tranſcribers and printers) than in Warburton's edition, where ſo much critical acumen is ſo ill directed ; or in Johnſon's firſt edition, in which, perhaps, there is not a ſingle faulty paſſage corrected, or difficult one explained. Farmer's eſſay is the moſt ſatisfactory piece of criticiſm that has yet appeared on Shakeſpeare ; and if

other

other critics had equal merit in thofe parts which are not included in that defign, there would be nothing left to defire for making a correct and compleat edition of this great author.

LETTER

LETTER XXIII.

TASTE, like wit, was never fatis-
factorily defined, although every one
knows, or fancies he knows, what it is.
I will not add to the number of defini-
tions, left mine fhould be alfo unfatis-
factory and prejudice my doctrine; but
I will endeavour, by a few unconnected
obfervations, to give my ideas on this
difficult fubject.

The term tafte, no doubt, was originally taken from the fenfation of the
palate; it is now equally applied to that
faculty of the mind which diftinguifhes
what is elegant. Its progrefs is the fame
in both: for, as the palate is at firft only
affected by powerful fenfations, and
after-

afterwards grows delicate; fo the mental
tafte in the beginning relifhes nothing
but violent impreffions, and afterwards
becomes refined. Refinement produces
the fame effects both in our corporeal and
mental tafte—it makes us reject what
we once approved.

Tafte then is not a gift from nature,
but an acquirement of art—nor is it
eafily acquired. Much attention and
application are requifite before we can be
truly faid to poffefs this quality. A long
and thorough acquaintance with the beft
authors ancient and modern, forms the
tafte for the Belles Lettres—and being
converfant in the works of the great
mafters, forms the tafte for the Polite
Arts. It is neceffary to know how the
moft diftinguifhed perfons have thought
on thefe fubjects, before we can be fure
of the truth of our own principles.

Yet, it is certain that all thefe circum-
,ftances

ftances united, will not alone confer
tafte—there muft be an aptitude to receive
the impreffion, which does not more
depend on ourfelves, than on the period
in which we live. The Englifh writers
and artifts a hundred and fifty years fince,
tho' they had the fame claffic authors to
read, and the fame ancient works of art
to ftudy as we have, yet were as deficient
in tafte as if thefe models of perfection
had not exifted.

Shakefpeare and Milton had not tafte
—the fineft paffages of thefe great poets
are very fuperior to any that writers of
a polifhed age *can* produce; but they are
fuch as no writer of a polifhed age *would*
produce : for tafte equally tends to abate
extreme beauties, and great faults.

As a barbarous age is not the period
for tafte, fo a refined ftate of fociety is
not the æra of genius. An Epic Poem
can never be again produced, poffeffing
the

the true characteriftic of that fpecies of compofition. It may be regular and beautiful like the Æneid, but not vehement and tranfporting like the Iliad.

Had not the civil wars interrupted the refinement that was dawning in the beginning of the reign of Charles the firft, the Paradife Loft would not have been fo grand—would not have been fo mean. Voltaire's objections to this poem, are, for the moft part, juft—they are the objections of a man of tafte to the productions of a man of genius. Upon the fame principle, Goldfmith remarked, that Shakefpeare's plays would not be endured if they were modern performances.

Voltaire always prefers Virgil to Homer, becaufe the poem of the former is more refined, and more confonant to his own elegant ideas than that of the latter. The Æneid was compofed when

tafte

taſte was at its height in Rome, and of courſe it is beautiful and faultlefs: the Iliad was produced before taſte exiſted in Greece, and for that reaſon it is bold and incorrect. If Virgil had poſſeſſed Homer's genius, the times in which he lived would not have permitted a poem like the Iliad—he would not have dared to expreſs ſuch bold ideas had he conceived them—and if Homer's had been the age of taſte, his fire inſtead of blazing, might never have kindled.

Taſte was much farther advanced in Italy when Taſſo writ his Gieruſalemme Liberata, than it was in England when Milton compoſed his Paradiſe Loſt; which accounts for the different character of the two poems. The latter has great faults and tranſcendent beauties— the former ſeldom riſes much above mediocrity, but never ſinks below it.

The early and great progreſs of taſte in
France

France has long incapacitated every poet of that country for any epic production. It is not the want of genius, but the state of fociety which renders it impoffible to produce a work whofe characteriftic is fire and fublimity. The Henriade pof-feffes the elegance of a polifhed age, not the irregular boldnefs of barbarous times. I have purpofely given a variety of in-ftances more firmly to eftablifh what I have advanced.

When writers of a refined age affect the ftyle of barbarous antiquity, they fhould firft diveft themfelves of tafte—the im-poffibility of doing this inftantly difco-vers the cheat. If this principle had been confidered, a difpute which fome time fince much engaged the public at-tention would foon have been ended; for an affectation of ancient orthography, and a few old words with new applica-tions, would never have weighed a mo-ment againft modern phrafeology, mo-dern modern manners, and modern facts. What has exifted may be imitated, but nothing lefs than the gift of prefcience can dive into futurity.—If it be improbable that an uneducated lad fhould be able to produce what are called Rowley's Poems, it is impoffible that Rowley could write with tafte, and allude to facts of after times.

Tafte has not only abated our genius, but it has alfo foftened our behaviour, and had its effect upon moft circumftances in life. Every thing that fhews a boldnefs of feeling is fubdued—all peculiarities that mark diftinction are avoided; fo that perfons are nearly on a level in company, tho' their talents may be materially different. Endeavours to excel are rather repreffed, for we avoid thofe fubjects with which we are moft acquainted, efpecially if profeffional, that we may not be thought pedants.

Sterne

Sterne was a prodigy.—By daring to
think for himfelf, and, what is more,
daring to exprefs his thoughts, he naturally belongs to a different period of fociety than that in which he lived—But
it is worthy obfervation, how every thing
in him like learning, is brought down
and familiarized by the manner in which
he writes. The deep philofopher, to
efcape fufpicion, appears as a fhallow
jcfter.—" Ufing his folly like a ftalk-
ing horfe, and under the prefentation of
that, fhoots his wit *."

We may conclude then, that by the
progrefs of tafte all great exertions of
genius are repreffed ; but that we have
gained in correctnefs and elegance, what
we have loft in force and fublimity.

* This was written before the publication of his
Plagiaries from Burton, &c. but they do not affect
this part of his character.

LETTER

LETTER XXIV.

I Cannot agree with you in the caufe of that uncommon production you mention ; my idea of this fubject, and on fome others connected with it, will appear by the following reflections.

Until the laft hundred years or thereabout, it was fuppofed that in many inftances life was produced by putrefaction, fermentation, &c. Leuwenhoek and other naturalifts, clearly demonftrated that fome animals, which were fuppofed to owe their exiftence to the above caufes, or in other words, to fpontaneous generation, had really a regular production. This difcovery eftablifhed the general principle of *omnia ab ovo*— but it muft be received with referve and exception.

After

After giving every theory of the earth a patient reading, it feems to me probable that the whole world was originally covered with water to the depth of about three miles, which is about as much below the furface, as the higheft mountains rife above it. This depth, though far below all foundings, bears no more proportion to the earth's diameter, than that of the paper it is covered with, does to a common globe. The idea of the fea approaching the center, and of courfe poffeffing a fuperior fhare in quantity, as well as furface of the earth, has occafioned many difficulties in accounting for the balance between the different fides of the globe; which vanifh, if the fea is not fuppofed of a greater depth than neceffity requires, or reafon and probability warrant.

I confider all continents as a congeries of iflands heaved up from the bottom of the

the fea by different caufes *. Modern
philofophers have difcovered ancient vol-
canos where they were never fufpected
to have exifted; and the whole earth is
full of evidence that it was once beneath

* Iflands feem to owe their origin to three different caufes—diftinct volcanic elevations—banks of
coral—or pieces of land feparated from the continent. Iflands of a pyramidal form, or confifting of
many fugar-loaf hills, belong to the firft fpecies—
the flat iflands in the South Sea to the fecond—and
to the third, Terra del Fuego in South America,
Ceylon in the Eaft Indies; and, to come nearer
home, the Ifle of Wight, the Weftern Ifles of Scotland, Ireland, and even Great Britain itfelf; all
which perhaps were once part of the continent. In
the fame manner as the fea has feparated the Weftern Ifles of Scotland; it is at this inftant working
its way through other pieces of land, which, in
time, will become iflands. The ingenious Mr.
Mills obferves, that the maps place the fituation of
the Weftern Ifles different from the truth. The fact
is, that the fea has encroached fo far as to demolifh
the old boundaries and headlands. He mentions
cliffs that are fallen, and others about to follow:
which is the cafe with the South-Weft coaft of Ireland as well——But this fubject, if purfued, would
lead me too far.

the

the ocean. Marble, freeftone, and many other fubftances, abound in fea-fhells
and marine productions. Some imagine
that the fea has left many places which
it once covered. Is it not rather to be
fuppofed that thefe places have been elevated above the fea, than that the fea has
funk below them? There feems to be no
caufe in nature equal to altering the quantity of water in the ocean, but we know
that there are many caufes by which the
land may be elevated. If the fea had
retired from the land, the retiring muft
have been equal in all places; this we
are fure is not the cafe, therefore it is the
land in that particular place that muft
have been raifed.

In the manner I fuppofe all land to
have been firft brought to light, many
iflands have been produced in our own
time, particularly in the range between
Vefuvius and Ætna—fome in the neigh-
bourhood of Iceland, and coral banks

without

without number. What was under the water is forced above it. The marine substances on the surface by degrees decay; moss appears, grass succeeds, then the smaller kind of plants, bushes, and trees *. Animal life begins and goes on upon the same scale from the minuter, to beings of more consequence †. This system is at least as general as the other,

* " By foaking of frequent showers, and the course of waters from the higher into lower grounds, when there is no issue, the flat land grows to be a mixture of earth and water, which is called a marsh. The higher, and fo the drier, parts, moistened by the rain, and warmed by the fun, shoot forth fome forts of plants, as naturally as bodies do hair, which being preferved by the defolatenefs of a place untrodden, grow to such trees or shrubs as are natural to the foil, and those in time producing both food and shelter for several kind of beasts, make what we call a forest." Sir W. Temple.

† It is remarkable that this idea of the order of production agrees with the succession of organized beings in the Mofaic account of the Creation.—It is the more remarkable, as the author was unconscious of the coincidence.

2   but

but, like that, muft be received with many reftrictions; for it is certain that by far the greater part of vegetables and animals would never be found indigenous or felf-produced in any one place, tho' many might live, and indeed flourifh, if brought thefe from the fpots where they firft had exiftence *.

Let

* Similar caufes produce like effects.—Thus a lake on a mountain in Scotland fhall have the fame fort of fifh in it as one in parallel circumftances in Switzerland, or any other mountainous country, where all variety arifing from latitude is made the fame by different elevations.—The char is found in lakes a thoufand leagues afunder, and it is ágreed that thefe fifh cannot be tranfported from the water of their birth to another—if they could, who is to do it ?—Plants are upon the fame principle, and are indigenous in places equally circumftanced. Mr. Saunders, who travelled from Bengal to Thibet, found on the mountains the fame plants as would be produced in like fituations in Europe, even to the commoneft weeds; among a great number, the arbutus uva urfi is mentioned, which is a native of Scotland, of the Alps, and Canada.—It fhould be remarked, that thefe mountains ftand in countries in

N 2   which

Let us proceed from reafoning to facts. Some voyager difcovers an ifland evidently, formed by a volcano, and very remote from other countries; it is a perfect wood to the water's edge, has fome plants which exift no where but in that fpot, together with others common to places in the fame latitude. It is full of infects, reptiles, birds, and fometimes quadrupeds. Now, if *every one* of thofe organized bodies was not brought there, fomething muft be felf-produced, or there muft be an after-act of creation for that particular fpot.

In fome iflands of the Eaft-Indies are ferpents of an enormous fize; who could carry them there? In all ftreams are fifh —how could they get there? Not from the fea, for fifh which inhabit the fource

which none of thefe plants are to be found, fo that the idea of feeds being wafted by the winds from one place to another cannot in thefe inftances be fuppofed.

of

of rivers are as foon killed by falt water as in air, befides there are many rivers which do not run into the ocean *. Perhaps this circumftance was never fufficiently confidered. Every fet of rivers is perfectly diftinct from any other fet. The greater number have fome fifh that exift no where but in the particular ftream in which they are bred. Pools of rain in warm countries prefently fwarm with fifh. Many animals and plants exift only in one fpot, if the place of their habitation be peculiar—fuch as the gigantic fnails of a fountain in Abyffinia, the crabs of another fountain near the Cape, and more particularly ftill, the fifh that inhabit the boiling ftreams which iffue from Mount Hecla. Find any other caufe for their firft production than what muft be taken from the old philofophy; for if they exift no where elfe, there is

---

* In Perfia are many rivers abounding in fifh, which are all exhaufted in watering grounds.

no place from whence they can be brought.

Let us attend to what we have always near us. Fill a veſſel with water from the pump: it is pure, and contains neither animal, nor vegetable. After ſtanding ſome days, a green ſubſtance begins to be formed in it, and which is afterwards inhabited by myriads of little beings : this ſeems the firſt ſtep towards plants and animals. We are told indeed that the animalcules are from eggs laid by flies, and the green ſlime is a plant which has its proper ſeed. That the water may accidentally receive both eggs and ſeed is highly probable ; but theſe (by reaſoning from other inſtances) ſeem the firſt efforts towards vegetable and animal life. Beſides, it yet remains to be proved, that the air ſo abounds with flying ſeeds and inſects. If the air ſwarmed, as is ſuppoſed, viſion would be obſtructed (as by a fog, which con-

ſiſts

fifts of particles inconceivably fmall),
and perhaps life, in the nobler animals,
deftroyed. The flime to be produced
from feed then muft have come from
fome of the fame fort in the neighbour-
hood; befides, if its being produced in
the water depended upon accident, which
it does by this fuppofition, it muft fometimes fail. Again, if the animals and
vegetables, in the above inftance, were
from eggs floating in the air, why are
the fmalleft always produced firft? Muft
it not fometimes happen that ova of a
larger fort would precede the fmaller?
which is never the cafe : not to mention
the total impoffibility of fome ova, particularly of animals, being fo conveyed.

It is well known that by pepper-water,
and a variety of other mixtures, peculiar
animalcules are produced. Can we fuppofe that the fly, which lays the egg
from which this creature exifts, con-
tinues floating in the air until fome philofopher

lofopher makes a mixture proper for its depofit ? Is it done often enough to preferve the fpecies ? What muft the fly have done before pepper was brought from India ? You may tell me that the egg was depofited there—well then, if the eggs are not hurt by the pepper being dried in an oven, happen to be brought to Europe, and fall in the way of a naturalift, the fpecies is preferved. Much is not got by this. There is great reafon for believing that the animalcule was really produced by the infufion, and did not exift before.

How are the worms in human bodies to be accounted for ? There are fome, no doubt, which bear an outward refemblance to earth-worms, and are fuppofed to be eggs we take in with roots, vegetables, &c. Not to infift upon the impoffibility of a creature intended to live in the cold earth exifting in the hot ftomach, it is an invariable rule in the animal

animal œconomy for the ftomach to di-
geft or rejeét every thing that it receives.
Animals when fwallowed alive, do not
remain fo long, but are inftantly begun to
be digefted. No animal can live in the
ftomach that ever lived out of it ; befides
we well know that there are worms in
the inteftines which have no refemblance
to any other thing in the creation—the
jointed worm, for inftance, which is
found of many yards in length. Where
does this animal exift except in the ftomach where it is found ? Sheep, dogs,
horfes, &c. breed worms peculiar to
themfelves*. I have feen frequently between the found and back-bone of a whit-
ing, long-worms that were evidently bred
there. Having no fyftem to fupport, I
fhall not objeét to your accounting for

* There was lately found in the aqueous humour
of a horfe's eye a creature unlike any other—previous
to the difcovering a paffage for the egg to fuch an un-
likely place, the exiftence of the parent itfelf is neceffary.

. thefe

thefe facts according to the prefent philofophy—but to me it feems abfolutely
impoffible*.

If

* The following curious paffage from Atkins's
Voyage is fo much to the purpofe, that I muft not be
deterred by its length from inferting it.

" We killed three or four pelicans, and on opening their bodies, met with the fame circumftances.

" I. They had double ventricles that together
reached the length of their bodies ; to the bottom of
which were connected the fmall guts, about twice as
thick as a fmall goofe-quill.

" II. In the firft ventricle or craw, the fifh they
had fwallowed (feventy or more) the bignefs of
fmaller fprats, lay whole and unaltered.

" III. In the lower ventricle, thofe little fifh
changing to a paler colour, were, nigh the fund of
it mafhed and macerated, and (what was princi-
pally meant by reciting any obfervations) here alfo
the mafs or pulp had an intimate mixture of numbers of flender lively worms in it ; which to me was
a matter of fpeculation, for finding no fuch infects
in

If two people's agreeing in the fame
thing, without a communication of fen-

in the fmall fifh above, which I imputed at firft
might have been their prey, I concluded it here to
be the common accident of concoction, a certain
confequence of heat and putrefaction, which are
conquered by farther digeftion, and pafs into infen-
fibility again ; for the fmall guts after a little diftance from the ftomach had none, or rather made
part of a yellow chylous fubftance.

" Query. Whether other, or all creatures have not
fuch a principle of concoction more or lefs difcernible
in fome than others ; though imperceptible, and differently fhaped and coloured, as the nature of the
food fwallowed, and the ftrength and heat of the
animal fwallowing ?"

Upon this account I would remark, that as the
worms appeared in the fame place, in the fame circumftances in all the birds, it may be inferred that
they were not accidental, but made part of the œconomy of the animal.

That their not being found above or below one
particular fpot, evidently fhews that they have their
exiftence only there.—For if they had been part of
the fifh, like them they would have been digefted.

timents,

timents, be a prefumption for its truth;
I can produce you a paffage from Dr.
Tyfon (as I find it in the Philofophical
Tranfactions), whofe authority will be a
ftrong fupport to what I have advanced.
—" The curious refearches of many in-
quifitive perfons after the manner of the
generation of infects, and their difcove-
ries therein, have much advanced the
doctrine of *univocal generation*. Yet,
one great difficulty remains with me, how
to account for feveral of thofe that are
bred in animal bodies; not fuch as we
may fuppofe to be hatched from the eggs
of the like kind, that are received with
the food or otherways, *but thofe of which
we cannot meet with a parallel, or of the
fame fpecies out of the body, in the whole
world, as is known, befides.* I fhall only
inftance in two, the *Lumbricus Latus*,
and *Teres*, which remarkably differ from
any others out of the body, from whence,
or from the feed of the fame, it may be
any

any ways thought they may be propagated
in it *."

Every thing I have advanced on felf-
production may be ftrengthened with additional arguments, and thofe from inftances on the largeft fcale. The old and
new continents are two immenfe iflands.
You will get little by fuppofing them
once joined at Beyring's Straits. What
fhould induce thofe animals which are
never feen out of a hot climate, to travel
fo far North as the Strait between the continents? They do not approach it now.

---

* If I were difpofed to make quotations to this
purpofe, there are enough to be found in every
writer on thefe fubjects of the laft century, and in
many of the prefent, who were never ftigmatized as
materialifts, or fuppofed to want a proper fenfe of
religion for difcuffing a point of natural philofophy.
" In debates (fays the ingenious author of The
World) perhaps purely fpeculative, a perfon is obliged not only to defend the point in controverfy, but
even his underftanding and moral character, which
are united to the queftion by the *management of his
adverfaries.*"

Befides

Befides, has not each continent fome creatures peculiar to itfelf ? Did thofe in America come from countries where no fuch animals exift ? if they did not, and are found in America only—what is the fair conclufion ?

, When an inhabitant of the old conti- nent afks how America was peopled, why does the queftion ftop there ? how was it fupplied with vegetables and ani- mals? particularly river-fifh ; and whence came thofe creatures that exift no where elfe ? Pray what is to hinder an American from reverfing the queftion ? When did our people, he may fay, firft migrate and give inhabitants to the Eaftern world? What anfwer can be given to thefe quef- tions confiftent with the prefent fyftem of philofophy ?

There is fomething in the found of felf-production which feems like a con- tradiction. I mean nothing more by it, than

than that a vegetable or animal in many inftances, firft feems to exift by a different principle from that upon which the fpecies is afterwards continued. As the term does not exactly exprefs this, it may eafily be perverted from the fenfe in which I wifh to be underftood*.

By whatever means the univerfe was formed, there is nothing in this fenfe of felf-production that fhocks any fyftem of belief. If it were the pleafure of our Creator, that fome organized bodies fhould firft exift (and our fenfes affure us that they do fo exift) from a certain combination of circumftances, and their ex-

---

* And it has been fo perverted.—If I had ufed the term indigenous (which in fact means the fame thing) no fin or abfurdity would have been committed, becaufe *indigenous* is an admitted term for all *local productions*—but do we not here

> Compound for words we are inclin'd to,
> By damning thofe we have no mind to?

iftence

iftence be continued afterwards upon different principles; are we to fay that thofe
things are contrary to nature, becaufe
other organized bodies are not fo formed?
The Polypus poffeffes properties which
belong to no other Being that has come
to our knowledge. Muft its peculiarity
deftroy our belief that there is fuch a
creature? Muft we deny that it has fuch
wonderful properties, becaufe they do
not agree with the common principles of
life? It is eafier, and perhaps wifer, to
form our fyftem from what we really fee,
than from what we only fuppofe; efpecially if fuch fuppofitions contradict the
knowledge derived from experience.—
Perhaps we fhall find, that felf-production fhocks the imagination more or lefs
according to the *fize* of the thing produced. Who would not rather believe
that cheefe breeds mites, than that deferts
produce elephants? And yet, according
to our prefent philofophy, the one is as
poffible as the other.

If

If the confequences I have drawn from
thefe facts appear to you wrong, or the
facts themfelves ill-fupported—convince
me of my error, and the whole fhall be
retracted as freely as it is advanced by

Yours moft faithfully, &c.

LETTER

LETTER XXV.

THOUGH I hate to fet out upon the
principle of word-hunting, yet it always
gives me pleafure when by accident I can
trace the meaning of a word or phrafe to
its fource, and purfue it through its various changes to its prefent ftate. The
pleafure is ftill greater, to mark the gra-
dual refinement of language from obfcu-
rity and barbarifm, until it arrives at precifion and elegance. Our tongue, as
every one knows, is a compound of
many. The pains which William the
Conqueror took to graft his Norman
French upon it, fucceeded in many

in-

inftances*, and there are others where we may trace the dying away of the French by degrees, and the Englifh refuming its old place. Chaucer in his character of the Monk, fays

He was a lord full fat and *in good point.*

This is the remains of the French *embonpoint*, or as it was written then *en bon point.*—The phrafe was wearing out in Chaucer's time, the *en bon* being tranflated, and *point* preferved. Now, the whole is tranflated, and we fay in *good cafe*, or *plight.*—The original is alfo loft,

---

* From Caxton's Vegetius it appears that the following words were in ufe in the reign of Henry the feventh:—preu—droits—empryfed—entremete--volente--preyfed--juriftes--poyfaunt—propice—foyfon —domageable, &c.—Some of thefe continued to the time of Shakefpeare. Other words from their terminations feem to have been perfectly naturalized, fuch as femblably—orguillous, &c.

in

in " to make his beard;" and many
other inſtances which occur in our old
writers.

" The days are now a cock-ſtride
longer," ſay the country folks at Twelfth-
day—and many have been the conjectures
upon the derivation of this phrafe (fee
the Gentleman's Magazine). It is not
cock-ſtride, but cock's-tread. In the
country, *tread* is pronounced *trede*, (not
tred)——and in moſt of the Weſtern
counties, Devonſhire excepted, *ſtride* has
more of the *e* than *i* in its found.—But
the impoſſibility of expreſſing by any
known ſigns the different provincial mo-
difications of the found of the vowels,
has occafioned fome ſtrange miſtakes
when people of one county endeavour to
write down an expreſſion ufed in another.
Our old poets, who generally ufed the
dialect of the province where they re-
fided, and ſpelt as well as they could with
their

their own country vowels, have given birth to much laughable criticifm.

Help-mate is an odd corruption. In the Book of Genefis it is faid, " it is not good for man to be alone, I will make an help meet for him*"—that is, an help *proper* for him—*meet* is an adjective. But thefe two words, like the firft man and his help, foon became one, and of late have been corrected into *help-mate.*

As I was reading John Struys's voyages the other day, I thought I difcovered the original of the word, and perhaps of the · liquor, punch ; which, if I am right,

* " And furthermore, when that our Lord had created Adam our former father, he faied in this wife: It is not good to be a manne alone, make we an *helper* to himfelfe femblable." CHAUCER.——
" His Majefty (Charles the firft) became heir as well to his father's virtues as to his kingdoms ; God found out a companion *meet for him,* our gracious Queen, &c."
Speech of Lord-keeper FINCH.

has

has nothing to do with that diverting perfonage in puppet-fhews of the fame name, from whom it is ufually derived. Struys was at Gomroon in Perfia, where he fays, he drank—" A liquor much in ufe there, called *pale punfken*, being compounded of arak, fugar, and raifins, which is fo bewitching that they cannot refrain from drinking it." I really believe he *forgot* to mention the water—for how in fuch a climate as the fouthern part of Perfia it was poffible to drink undiluted arak, I have no conception. The raifins have given place, and very properly, to lemons. But I had better leave this to its own merits.—I am afraid it will not bear too minute an examination—remember it is only *humbly* offered together with the other conjectures of

Yours, &c.

As Struys's Voyages is a fcarce book, I might with great eafe have practifed

I   the

the common trick of authors, and introduced *water* into the quotation without fear of difcovery. It being fuppofed that few will give themfelves the trouble to turn to the original book to examine extracts; authors have been made to give evidence to facts, " of which they nothing know," and to fupport fyftems which never had exiftence, but in the imagination of the writer who preffes them into his fervice.

LETTER

LETTER XXVI.

ALLITERATION very early made
its appearance in Englifh poetry. I have
feen an old piece where it was intended
to fupply the place of rhyme : the terminations were different; but in every
line were three or four words which begun with the fame letter. This I fuppofe was thought a beauty.

Shakefpeare in feveral places bur-
lefques the improper ufe of Alliteration
with great pleafantry. He might dif-
countenance but he could not deftroy the
practice—

> The Floor, faithlefs to the fuddled foot,

of Thomfon, and

> His pray'r preferr'd to faints that cannot aid,
> His praife poftpon'd and never to be paid,

of Cowper

are

are fcarcely lefs ridiculous than Shakefpeare's

Bravely broach'd his bloody boiling breaſt.

I believe wherever alliteration is *perceived*,
it difguſts.

There is fomething very ridiculous in
the pains of an author, when he is
fearching for a fet of words beginning
with the fame letter: this furely argues
a " lack of matter." A man who has
things in his head, is never curious about
words, unlefs it be thofe which exprefs
his meaning quickly and with precifion *.

I dare

---

* The following paffage from Cotton's Tranſlation of Montaigne, feems to be the original of the
above remark, but the author had never read Montaigne when thefe letters were firſt publiſhed. This
may ferve as a proof, that two perfons may have
the fame thought, and, as in this inſtance, nearly
the fame expreffion. " I would have *things* fo exceed, and wholly poffefs the imagination of him that
fpeaks,

I dare fay it coft Smollet as much time
to fix upon the name *Roderick Random*,
as to write fome of the beft parts in that
fprightly and entertaining performance.
—*Robert* and *Richard* were common,
Roger and *Ralph* were vulgar—there was
a neceffity for a founding uncommon
name, and beginning with an *R:* at laft,
by a lucky chance *Roderick* occurred—
and *Roderick* it is.—Do you think me
fanciful? I call upon *Peregrine Pickle*,
and *Ferdinand Count Fathom* to prove the
contrary.

fpeaks, that he fhould have fomething elfe to do than
to think of *words*. The language that I love is natural and plain, as well in writing as in fpeaking,
and a finewy and fignificant way of expreffing a
man's felf—fhort and pithy, and not fo elegant and
artificial, as prompt and vehement." Again—" In
language to ftudy new phrafes and to affect words
that are not of current ufe, proceeds from a childifh
and fcholaftic ambition." There are two authors of
great diftinction, Johnfon and Gibbon, whofe ftyle
is formed upon principles directly oppofite to this
opinion of Montaigne.

If

If we laugh at the hard-fought-for Alliteration of the poet and hiftorian, may we not laugh a little louder at that of the comic dramatift? Can any language be lefs that of nature or common converfation, than ftrings of words beginning with an M or N? and ,yet this has been done by one who " paints the Manners living as they rife." It is furprifing that fo fprightly a genius as Foote, could fubmit to the drudgery of confulting his fpelling-book for words proper to be paired—my three *ppp*'s put me in mind of a letter in the Student, in which *p* is predominant; it feems to have been written to burlefque the abfurd practice of Alliteration, and is highly humorous and entertaining.

Will you give me leave to make an abrupt tranfition from Alliteration to *Literation*, and pardon me alfo for coining?

The

The Germans in pronouncing Englifh, and writing it too, if they have not ftudied the language, almoft conftantly change *b* into *p*, *d* into *t*, *g* (hard) into *k*, *v* into *f*, and the reverfe. This peculiarity of theirs, I find, upon recollection, is not confined to the Englifh. In the Burletta of *La buona Figliuola*, the author makes his German character to fay *trompetti* and *tampurri*; nay they ferve their own language the fame, as I have obferved from their pronunciation of proper names of cities, &c. It feems difficult to account for this; but perhaps not more fo, than for the trick of the French in giving an afpirate to thofe Englifh words where there is none, and omitting it where it fhould be ufed.

This is more excufable in them than the fame practice which has obtained with fome among ourfelves.—It is confined indeed to our own language; in any other we are not guilty of this incorrectnefs.

LETTER

THOUGH fuperftition is pretty well laughed away, yet in fome points it ftill exifts in full force. The wedding-ring in coffee grounds—the coffin in the candle—the ftranger in the fire, are marked by none but vulgar and foolifh eyes. You fee falt fpilt—hear death-watches— owls hoot—dogs howl, and defpife the omen—you are above it. But yet let me afk *you*, an enlightened philofopher— Whether you are above choice of feats at whift? Whether you have not really believed that your chance for winning was much bettered by taking the fortunate chairs, and of courfe obliging your adverfaries to fit not in thofe of the fcornful, but of the lofers? When you quit the game on a run of ill luck, what

is

is it but declaring your belief that the
games already played have an influence
upon thofe which are to come?

Each ticket in a lottery has an equal
chance—do you think fo? Number 1000
gained the great prize in the laft lottery—
now, confefs honeftly, that fomething
within tells you, the fame number can
never win the great prize again——you
would prefer every other number to it—
and yet reafon fays, that all the tickets
have an equal probability of fuccefs *.
In thefe inftances, and many others, fuperftition, even in cultivated minds, will
be always more than a match for truth.

A gentleman coming a paffenger in a
veffel from the Weft-Indies, finding it

* Some years fince a perfon divided the tickets of
a lottery into claffes—Thofe he ftiled fortunate, were
to have a fuperiority of prizes. His calculation was
formed upon rejecting the numbers which had been
fortunate in former lotteries.

more

more inconvenient to be fhaved than to wear his beard, chofe the latter—but he was not fuffered to have his choice long —it was the unanimous opinion of the failors, and indeed of the Captain as well, that there was not the leaft pro-bability of a wind as long as this omi-nous beard was fuffered to grow. They petitioned—they remonftrated, and at laft prepared to cut the fatal hairs by violence. Now, as there is no operation at which it is fo much the patient's intereft to con-fent, as that of the barber—the gentle-man quietly fubmitted—nor could the wind refift the potent fpell, which in-ftantly filled all their fails, and " wafted them merrily away."

You fee we have only got rid of *ge-neral* fuperftition, we ftill retain that which belongs to our particular profeffion or purfuits.

Adieu.

LETTER

LETTER XXVIII.

I Have often tried to have a proper conception of vaſt ſpace—great numbers—enormous ſize, and, as you may ſuppoſe, without ſucceſs. But though I fail in getting a competent idea, I ſometimes make an approach towards it, which is better than nothing.

The ſolar ſyſtem is one of theſe ſublime ſubjects, in the conſideration of which I have frequently been loſt. I never attempted to conceive the ſize of the ſun, or the diſtance of ſaturn; the impoſſibility inſtantly repels the moſt daring imagination. No, all that I have attempted is, to judge of the proportion (upon any ſcale) that the ſun and planets bear

bear to each other, in refpect to fize and diftance.

At firft fight, this feems eafily done— Draw fome concentric circles on a fheet of paper, make the fun the centre, and place the planets round in their order.— Or if you would have an idea of their motion alfo, look at an orrery. But a little examination will convince you, that this is doing nothing towards conceiving their fize and diftance in proportion to each other, which is the point fought. Nay, it is worfe than nothing, for it impofes a falfity as a reality. Imagination by itfelf can do a great deal, if affifted it can do more, but if perverted, nothing. Let us try then to affift the imagination.

If the fun be only a million times bigger than the earth, it is plain that I cannot make two circles upon a fheet of paper (without confidering any thing

about

about diftance) that will bear this proportion to each other; and if this cannot be done for the earth, much lefs will it ferve for other planets and moons, where the difproportion is greater.

Let us take the floor of a large room —on this make a circle of two feet diameter for the fun—the fize of the earth will be about a large pin's head. The diftance of the fun from the earth is about eighty of the fun's diameters; if fo, there muft be a circle of three hundred and twenty feet diameter for the earth's orbit, which no room, nor indeed any other building, will contain.

Let us try a field—here we may put our fun, and draw the earth's orbit round. If we ftand in the centre, (which we fhould do) the earth is too fmall to be feen. Thefe difficulties occurring fo foon, how will they encreafe when we take in the fuperior planets?

The

3

The ingenious Fergufon endeavoured to affift our imagination, by fuppofing St. Paul's dome, in diameter one hundred and forty-five feet, to be the fun—upon this fcale, Mercury is between nine and ten inches, and placed at the Tower; Venus near eighteen, at St. James's Palace; the Earth, eighteen, at Marybone; Mars ten, at Kenfington; Jupiter fifteen feet, at Hampton-Court; and Saturn eleven feet and half, at Cliffden. Let us be on the top of the dome, and look for the planets where he has placed them. Do you think we could fee any thing of Jupiter and Saturn? to fay nothing of their moons—or that we could conceive properly the difference between four miles and twenty, when feen on a line? the four may be two, or one mile; and the twenty may be ten, or thirty, for ought we can judge by the appearance. All that we gain by this is, the knowing that a fheet of paper, or an orrery, give us wrong ideas; and that we cannot, by

any

any contrivance, put the fize and diftance
of the planets upon a proportionable
fcale, fo as to take in the whole with,
our eye or underftanding *.

We are as much at a lofs to compre-
hend the flownefs of their motion—I
have not miftaken—I mean, flownefs.—
The performance of a circuit in fix or
twelve months, or twice as many years,
gives no idea of fwiftnefs; and yet
this motion is called whirling—as if the
planets went round their orbits like a
top ! Though quick and flow are comparative terms, we have ideas of each
arifing from the medium of the two,
from obfervation, and common application, that do not ftand in need of any
comparifon to be underftood. The motion of a flea is quick; of a fnail, flow;
and the common walk of a man is

---

* Thefe difficulties are encreafed very confiderably
by the difcovery of the new planet.

neither

neither quick nor flow. Let us imagine
an elephant to walk, and a flea to hop
the fame diftance in the fame time—
would you hefitate to fay that the motion
of the one was flow, and the other
quick? Swiftnefs or flownefs does not
depend upon the abfolute quantity of
ground the animal paffes in a certain
time, but upon the relative quantity to
its own fize.

The earth is about eight minutes in
moving the fpace of one diameter, therefore its abfolute motion is flow—it is
twenty-four hours making one revolution
round its axis, which gives no idea of,
velocity. It is certain that if we were
placed very near the earth (unaffected by
its attraction) there would appear an exceeding quick change of furface—and
fo would the motion of a fnail appear to
an animalcule. The quantity of fpace,
when compared to any we can move in
the fame time, is vaft, and the motion
quick;

quick; but when confidered as belonging
to a body of the fize of a world, the
motion is flow.

Suppofe a common globe was turned
round once in twenty-four hours—imagine an animal as much inferior to it in
fize as we are to the earth, placed, as I
conceived the human fpectator placed,
to view the earth—would the apprehen-
fion of this Being induce you to call a
fingle revolution in twenty-four hours,
whirling? Would not you fay, that
though the furface paffed fwiftly in re-
view before him, yet that the abfolute
motion of the whole was exceedingly
flow? Perhaps it is our meafuring the
planetary progrefs by miles, that makes
us conceive it to be quick; which is
much like taking the heighth of a mountain in hairs-breadths. When we are
told that Saturn moves in his orbit more
than twenty-two thoufand miles in an
hour, we fancy the motion to be fwift;
but

but when we find that he is more than three hours moving his own diameter, we muſt then think it as it really is, ſlow. Biſhop Wilkins is the only writer I have met with who confiders the motion of the heavenly bodies as I do, and I am rather proud of having my opinion ſupported by ſo great a man.

. There is another circumſtance which prevents the ſolar ſyſtem, as commonly delineated, from bearing a true reſemblance to the apparent poſition and motion of the planets. It is always drawn in plan inſtead of ſection, whereas the *appearance* of the orbits of the heavenly bodies is always in ſection, and never can be in plan. This difference is not, as far as I know, noticed in any account of the ſolar ſyſtem ; and yet if it be not attended to, it is impoſſible to prove the truth of the ſyſtem by the *apparent* paths of the planets.

This

This will be beſt underſtood by con‑ ſidering the inferior ones. Mercury and Venus remove to a certain diſtance from the ſun, and then, after ſeeming at reſt, they return in nearly the ſame line, and remove to the ſame diſtance on the other ſide, where the ſame thing is repeated. This to the eye is not a revolution in plan, but a revolution in ſection—and it might be explained by a draught which ſhould always accompany the common delineation of the planetary orbits.

LETTER

LETTER XXIX.

IT is fo long fince I fent you the firft part of my obfervations on Quarles, that perhaps you have forgot my promife for the remainder.—I will now refume the fubject.

Quarles fometimes introduces perfonages, and makes his poem of the dramatic caft. The fixth hieroglyphic is a dialogue between *Time* and *Death*; as ufual, alluding to the print, where *Death* is about to extinguifh the taper, but is prevented by *Time*. There are a few awkward expreffions in this, which may be more eafily overlooked than omitted.

Time.

Time.   Death.

Time. Behold the frailty of this slender snuff;
　　Alas! it hath not long to last;
　　Without the help of either chief or puff,
　　Her weaknefs knows the way to waste :
　　Nature hath made her substance apt enough
　　　To spend itself, and spend too fast :
　　　　It needs the help of none
　　　　.That is so prone
　　To lavish out untouch'd, and languish all alone.

Death. *Time,* hold thy peace, and shake thy slow-pac'd
　　　　　　　　　　　　　　　　[stand ;
　　　Thine idle minutes make no way ;
　　Thy glafs exceeds her hour, or else doth stand,
　　　I cannot hold, I cannot stay.
　　Surceafe my pleading, and enlarge my hand,
　　　I forfeit with too long delay ;
　　　　This brisk this bold-fac'd light
　　　　Doth burn too bright :
　　Darknefs adorns my throne, my day is darkest
　　　　　　　　　　　　　　　　　[night.

Time. Great Prince of darknefs! hold thy needlefs
　　　　　　　　　　　　　　　　　　[hand,
　　　Thy captive's fast and cannot flee ;
　　What arm can refcue ? who can countermand ?　.
　　　What pow'r can fet thy pris'ner free ?
　　Or if they could ; what clofe, what foreign land
　　　Can hide that head that flees from thee ?
　　　　　　　　　　　　　　　　　　　But

But if her harmlefs light
Offend thy fight
Why need'ft thou fnatch at noon, what muft be
[thine at night ?

Death. I have outftaid my patience ; my quick trade
Grows dull and makes too flow return;
This long-liv'd debt is due, and fhould been paid
When firft her flame began to burn :
But I have ftaid too long, I have delay'd
To ftore my vaft, my craving urn.
My patent gives me pow'r
Each day, each hour,
To ftrike the peafant's thatch, and fhake the
[princely tow'r.

Time. Thou count'ft too faft : thy patent gives no pow'r
Till Time fhall pleafe to fay, Amen.
Death. Canft thou appoint my fhaft ? *Time.* Or thou my
[hour ?
Death. 'Tis I bid, do. *Time.* 'Tis I bid, when ;
Alas ! thou canft not make the pooreft flow'r
To hang the drooping head 'till then :
Thy fhafts can neither kill,
Nor ftrike, until
My power gives them wings, and pleafure arms
[thy will.

There is nothing which deftroys the
reality in a dramatic dialogue more than
when the fpeakers afk queftions and reply
in

in an equal quantity of lines. Perhaps the moſt difguſting inſtance of this is in Milton's Maſk, where Comus and the Lady have a verſe each alternately, for fourteen lines together. We are more ſenſible of the ſameneſs in quantity where it is ſo ſhort, and ſo often repeated, than here in Quarles where it is extended to a ſtanza, and that repeated for each ſpeaker but once—but even here you begin to feel its bad effect, when it is finely relieved towards the end by the characters growing warmer in their diſpute, and, of courſe, making the ſpeeches ſhorter.

Yet, what I here condemn, others admire.—You, who are ſo fond of the ancients, may eaſily defend this practice by their example, and if you want any aſſiſtance to demoliſh me, may call in Mr. Weſt and the author of the Origin and Progreſs of Language.—The following paſſage of the former from his tranſlation of the Iphigenia of Euripedes

is

is quoted by the latter with great com-
mendations—not indeed becaufe the dialogue is in alternate verfe, but becaufe it
is a fine imitation of the ancient trochaic
meafure.

Iph. Know'ft thou what fhould now be ordered?
  Tho. 'Tis thy office to prefcribe.
Iph. Let them bind in chains the ftrangers.
  Tho. Canft thou fear they fhould efcape?
Iph. Truft no Greek; Greece is perfidious.
  Tho. Slaves depart, and bind the Greeks.
Iph. Having bound, conduct them hither, &c.

It is true that here the reply wants one
of having the fame number of fyllables
as the queftion—but ftill, the conftant return of the fame quantity for each fpeaker
is difagreeable to all unprejudiced ears.—
You will tell me that it is in the high
gufto of the antique, and that the feet
are trochaics—I can only reply, that hard
words cannot convince me when contrary
to reafon, and if a proper effect be not
produced, it is of very little confequence
to me whether the authority be brought
from

Greece or Siberia. Horace's often-quoted *Pallida mors*, &c. was perhaps never better tranflated than at the end of the fourth ftanza.

The ninth hieroglyphic will put you in mind of the poems that are fqueezed or ftretched into the form of axes, altars, and wings—but if you will attend to the matter and not the form, you will find it excellent—to write this properly requires fome care.

Behold
How fhort a fpan
Was long enough of old
To meafure out the life of man;
In thofe well-temper'd days, his time was then
Survey'd, caft up, and found but three-fcore years and ten!

Alas!
And what is that?
They come, and flide, and pafs,
Before my pen can tell thee what.
The pofts of Time are fwift, which having run
Their fev'n fhort ftages o'er, their fhort-liv'd tafk is done.

Our

Our days
Begun, we lend!
To fleep, to antick plays
And toys, until the firft ftage end;
12 waining moons twice 5 times told, we give
To unrecover'd lofs : we rather breathe than live.

We fpend
A ten years breath
Before we apprehend
What 'tis to live, or fear a Death :
Our childifh dreams are fill'd with painted joys
Which pleafe our fenfe awhile, and waking prove but toys!

How vain
How wretched is
Poor man, that doth remain
A flave to fuch a ftate as this !
His days are fhort, at longeft ; few at moft;
They are but bad at beft ; yet lavifh'd out, or loft.

They be
The fecret fprings
That make our minutes flee
On wheels more fwift than eagle's wings ?
Our life's a clock, and every gafp of breath
Breathes forth a warning grief, till Time fhall ftrike a Death!

How foon
Our new-born light
Attains to full-ag'd noon!
And this, how foon to grey-hair'd night !
We fpring, we bud, we bloffom and we blaft
E'er we can count our days, our days they flee fo faft!
They

They end
When fcarce begun!
. And e'er we apprehend
That we begin to live, our life is done:
Man count thy days; and if they fly too faft
For thy dull thoughts to count, ·count ev'ry day the laft.

Methinks Quarles's ghoft is at my el-
bow, and will not be appeafed unlefs I
remark that the firft lines of each ftanza
make a verfe, being the text on which the
poem is a comment.

*Behold, alas! our days we fpend:
How vain they be, how foon they end!*

This is a kind of falfe wit once much in
requeft, particularly in Spain. In Don
Quixote is a poem of this fort which is
called by the tranflator a Text and Glofs.
It differs however from Quarles's, the
text being introduced at the end, and not
at the beginning of the ftanza.

It is impoffible to avoid fmiling at the
pains he muft have taken to preferve the
form

form of the ftanza—in the third he is obliged to have the affiftance of figures, or his line would have been too long; and after all his trouble, there muft be fome for the reader before he has calculated the amount of " twelve moons, twice five. times told :" in the reft, to fay the truth, it is not fo apparent. If this pyramidical ftanza prevent you from attending to the poetry, it is eafily put in another—of the two firft lines make one; and the falfe wit immediately vanifhes.——I hope Quarles's ghoft vanifhed before I propofed the alteration.

I have, like a prudent caterer, referved the beft thing for the laft. It is the twelfth emblem of the third book. The fubject of the print is a figure trying to efcape from the divine vengeance which is purfuing in thunders: the motto— *O that thou wouldft hide me in the grave, that thou wouldft keep me in fecret until thy wrath be paft!* Upon this hint he

has

has produced the following excellent
poem.

*Ah! whither shall I fly? what path untrod
Shall I seek out to 'scape the flaming rod
Of my offended, of my angry God?

Where shall I sojourn? what kind sea will hide
My head from thunder? where shall I abide,
Until his flames be quench'd or laid aside?

What if my feet should take their hasty flight,
And seek protection in the shades of night?
Alas! no shades can blind the God of light.

What if my soul should take the wings of day,
And find some desert? if she spring away,
The wings of vengeance clip as fast as they.

What, if some solid rock should entertain
My frighted soul? can solid rocks restrain
The stroke of Justice and not cleave in twain?

*Mr. Cowper seems to have felt the force of these
animated lines, by the following imitation:

Oh, for a shelter from the wrath to come;
Crush me ye rocks, ye falling mountains hide,
Or bury me in Ocean's angry tide.—

Nor fea, nor fhade, nor fhield, nor rock, nor cave,
Nor filent deferts, nor the fullen grave,
Where flame-ey'd fury means to fmite, can fave.

'Tis vain to flee; 'till gentle mercy fhew
Her better eye; the farther off we go,
The fwing of Juftice deals the mightier blow.

Th' ingenuous child, corrected, doth not flie
His angry mother's hand, but clings more nigh,
And quenches with his tears her flaming eye.

Great God! there is no fafety here below;
Thou art my fortrefs, thou that feem'ft my foe,
'Tis thou that ftrik'ft the ftroke, muft guard the blow.

Six ftanzas, which though very good, yet being of lefs merit than the reft are omitted. It is obvious that he had the 139th pfalm in his eye, of which he has made great ufe. The alarm at the beginning—the fearching all nature for fhelter—the impoffibility of being hid from the author of nature—and the acquiefcing at laft in what was unavoidable, are grand and natural ideas. The motion of the

Q 2   wings

wings of vengeance—and the recapitula-
tion of the places where protection was
fought in vain—are inftances of expreffion rarely met with. But what praife is
fufficient for the fimile in the eighth
ftanza? To fay only that it is appofite
and beautiful, comes very fhort of my
fenfations when I read it. Let me confefs honeftly, that I think it one of the
nobleft inftances of the fublime pathetic!
As a part of a religious poem it is proper,
in a high degree; the fcripture frequently
confidering our connection with the Al-
mighty as that of children with a parent.
—As a pictorefque image it is diftinct,
natural, and affecting.—But to remark
all the beauties of this poem would be to
comment on every ftanza.—You will have
more pleafure in finding them out yourfelf.

Now what think you, is not this rather too good to be loft?

Was

Was it from the number of falfe thoughts
and the many inftances of falfe wit in
which Quarles fo much abounds, that
Pope had not patience to fearch for his
beauties? and it is certain they are but
few in proportion to his faults. It is not
my intention to fay more in his favour
than may be defended by quotation. I
think my praifes ftrongly fupported, but
I do not expect that they will have fufficient
force to turn a tide of abufe which has
been flowing againft this poet for more
than an hundred years.

P, S. I fhould have informed you
that thefe emblems were imitated in Latin
by one Herman Hugo, a Jefuit. The
firft edition of them was in 1623, foon
after the appearance of Quarles; and the
book was reprinted for the ninth time in
1676, which laft is the date of the copy
in my poffeffion. How many more editions there have been I know not. He
makes no acknowledgment to Quarles,
and

and fpeaks of his own work as original.
As a fpecimen of his manner, take the
following, which is intended as an imitation of " Ah whither fhall I fly ?"

> Quis mihi fecuris dabit hofpita tecta latebris ?
> Tecta, quibus dextræ ferver ab igne tuæ ?
> Heu ! tuus ante oculos quoties furor ille recurfat,
> Nulla mihi toties fida fat antra reor.

> Tunc ego fecretas, umbracula frondea, fylvas,
> Luftràque folivagis opto relicta feris.
> Tunc ego vel mediis timidum caput abdere terris,
> Aut maris exesâ condere rupe velim, &c.

It reads but poorly after the other, though
I have given you the beft paffages. He
afterwards by degrees quits his fubject,
runs into ftuff about Cain and Jonah, and
has entirely omitted the fimile,

LETTER

LETTER XXX.

FIVE hundred years fince, old Hodge
Bacon (as Butler calls him) wrote a
treatife, *De Impedimentis Sapientiæ*—perhaps, he had to complain, in common
with authors of a more modern date,
that the rubs and difficulties which the
public throw in the way of genius at its
firſt appearance, are frequently too great
to be furmounted.

We are apt to form our opinion of
abilities by their refemblance to thofe by
which fame has already been acquired.
A painter, a mufician, or an author perfectly new, we are afraid to commend—
like hounds, we wait for the opening of
one whofe cry we may venture to follow.
We have a reputation to lofe by com-
mending

mending in the wrong place; and we
have a reputation to gain by seeing some-
thing to censure that is unperceived by
the common eye—We have prepossessions
to overcome, old opinions to unfix, and
new ones to establish, before we can
fairly judge of *original* merit: and as
this merit (to which I entirely confine the
remark) is always accompanied with
modesty, the possessor, instead of finding
that encouragement and protection his
abilities seem to demand, passes his life
neglected, and is left to languish in
hopeless obscurity.

The greatest part of those who seem
to have been born to make mankind happy, were themselves miserable. If we
know any thing of Homer, it is, that
he wandered through Greece reciting his
verses like a modern ballad-singer.—
Wretched, unhappy, half-starved Cer-
vantes, Camöens, Butler, Fielding!
Does it not grieve one to hear that the

author

author of Tom Jones lies in the Factory's burying ground at Lifbon, undiftinguifhed, unregarded—not a ftone to mark the place * ! while we behold ftately memorials erected to fome, who have done nothing to deferve, or who fhould have fhunned the public attention —to others, who from fome lucky concurrence of circumftances, have had credit with their contemporaries for abilities and virtues, which will not be acknowledged by pofterity—and to others, whofe very names were fecret until they appeared in their epitaphs. Fortunately, thefe ill-merited diftinctions are foon loft, and are rather confidered as monuments to the fame of the fculptor, than of the perfons whofe duft they fo pompoufly cover.

The inftances of thofe original ge-

* It is faid that the Members of the Royal Academy of Lifbon have lately ordered a monument to his memory.

niufes,

nuifes, who in their life-time have en-
joyed the applaufe of the public, and
lived by it, are very few—indeed I cannot recollect any—Garrick excepted. I
do not confider Virgil or Pope in this
light—they are not original. It is true
that Shakefpeare lived well enough ; but
the money he gained was by acting, not
writing. Milton was in tolerable circumftances ; but if his whole dependence
had been on the profit arifing from the
fale of the fineft poem in the world, he
muft have been ftarved.

The Biographia Britannica is to me
the moft pathetic book in our language.
If it record the learning and genius of
many of our countrymen, it records alfo
their difappointments, their poverty, their
mifery, and the fpurns inflicted on them
by the unworthy. As fure as you read
the life of a man celebrated for his abilities, fo certain you find that he had to
combat with the world's oppreffion and
perfecution ;

perfecution; as if the interefts of mankind were concerned in ftifling a flame that would light them to virtue, knowledge, and happinefs.

The mournful fenfations arifing from furveying tombs in the repofitories of the dead, are pleafant when compared to what I feel on entering a large library; which I confider as a vaft collection of monuments to trouble and unrewarded merit. When I reflect on the labour neceffary to produce the moft inconfiderable volume, and multiply it by the whole number of books before me, I am loft under fuch an accumulation of human mifery! Perhaps, out of the thoufands of authors which my eye fo quickly glances over, not fifty had any other reward in their life-time, than amufing their imagination with vain notions of pofterity beftowing the fame which was denied by their contemporaries. An author's firft ideas undoubtedly

are

are prefent rewards; but he foon finds,
that though death feems not effential to
reputation, yet that life is too fhort to
eftablifh it. Impreffed with thefe me-
lancholy ideas, he exclaims with the
Poet—

> But the fair Guerdon when we hope to find,
> And think to burft out into fudden blaze,
> Comes the blind fury with th' abhorred fhears,
> And flits the thin-fpun life!——

THE END.